To John,
10/12/

GW00866388

The
Solstice
Blade

Rob Beck

MANDOLIN
PRESS

Cover design by Spiffing Covers

www.spiffingcovers.com

ISBN-13: 978-0-9956734-1-0

Printed by TJ International Ltd, Padstow, Cornwall

DEDICATION

For my sons and everyone searching for the magic that has
gone missing from the world.

CONTENTS

ACKNOWLEDGMENTS

I would like to thank the following individuals for the help
and support during the creation of this novel:
My sons for providing me with a reason to write and the
inspiration for most of the ideas in this book.
Paula, my inspiration for almost everything else.
Kym Kippax, Jason Longhorn, Gareth Dudley and Jess
Hoggett for reviewing the various incarnations of the
manuscript.

1 PROLOGUE

The ancient horseman laughed with feral glee as the lightning bolt hit him. The current surged through his body shaking his bones just as it had done a thousand times before. Screwing up his wind-burned face, he urged his mount forward through the storm, oblivious to the driving rain that soaked through the scorched, tattered rags that had once been his clothes.

Far below, between the scudding shredded remnants of rain-clouds, movement on the ground drew his eye.

With a well practiced deftness at odds with his apparent age, he twisted his horse's cracked leather reins around his hand and, bracing himself against the saddle with his legs, he leaned precariously outwards into thin air. Looking down towards the distant earth, dark and forbidding under the cover of the storm, he glimpsed his quarry.

Several hundred feet below, a terrified woman scrambled and slipped over the granite boulders that were strewn across the barren uplands of Bodmin Moor. Still wearing her traditional bal maiden's outfit after a day spent working at the surface of one of the local copper mines, she was easy to spot from the air. Her white gook, the protective bonnet that female mine workers used to cover their heads and shoulders, stood out clearly against the drab greens and greys of the moor.

With the slightest tensing of his knees, the rider guided his horse into a steep dive.

Sensing that she had been seen, Chastity Trewartha risked a panicked glance upwards over her shoulder. Behind her, against a backdrop of boiling black storm-clouds, a host of horsemen accompanied by a pack of baying hounds poured down out of the sky towards her in a scene from a nightmare. With an ear-splitting crack, like the pillars of heaven collapsing, another bolt of lightning arced out of the clouds into the lead rider's corroded crown and exploded out through the tip of his sword seeking an exit to earth. For a moment, in the intense illumination of the lightning bolt, time appeared to stand still and everything was frozen in place: The wild excitement in the man's eyes as the electricity blasted through him; his horse's rain-sodden mane whipping through the air before him; the tendrils and filaments of blue-white light that danced around his sword blade as the current passed through - all these things were burned into Chastity's memory. In a split second it was over, time regained its usual pace, and the hoard screamed earthward.

Chastity ran on in blind panic, terror clouded her reasoning, but reason had no place in this situation. Instead, it drove her forward in a flow-state outside of her conscious control. Driven by fear Chastity vaulted effortlessly over boulders that ordinarily she would have had trouble even clambering over. Decisions as to which was the quickest and safest route around the many rain filled pits were instantly made, and were acted on without hesitation.

Despite this however, she knew that they were gaining on her. Then, with a rush of relief, she saw her salvation; in the distance, misted and blurred by the rain, she could make out the familiar dark, looming mass of a mine engine. Incongruously, given her current situation, she noticed for the first time how the buildings, with their high narrow engine houses, and long tapering chimneys looked like giant hands with one finger pointing at the sky, a warning that had almost come too late for her.

With renewed energy fuelled by the hope of escape, Chastity raced to the shelter of the mine engine, but within a few steps her clothing, that served her so well during her working day, protecting her from the excess of the weather, conspired against her. Her heavy skirt and apron, waterlogged from the downpour, clung to her legs and snagged on low gorse bushes making each step more laborious than the last.

The sound of Chastity's heartbeat pounded in her ears with the exertion of her escape, and each gasping breath rasped painfully through her throat, as she closed the gap between herself and the safety of the building. But as she drew nearer the rhythmic thumping of her pulse was rapidly overwhelmed by a deep rumbling that she could feel through the earth beneath her feet. Chastity recognised the familiar tattoo of hoofbeats; her pursuers were on the ground. The shaking of the earth increased until suddenly she found herself flanked on either side by the lead hounds of the spectral hunt. Rather than attacking, the dogs kept pace with her, howling and barking with the excitement of the chase, and were joined as they ran by more and more of their kind. Behind her, she could hear the unearthly whoops and calls of the riders as they gained on her. In desperation, Chastity ripped off her sodden gook, and flung it at one of the hounds. The animal yelped in surprise, and veered away, but was instantly replaced. Unfortunately, the action was enough to take her attention away from the ground for just long enough for her to miss her footing and fall forward. At the last moment, she brought her hands up to protect her face from the imminent impact with a rough granite Boulder. She need not have bothered, for she never hit the ground: With a sickening lurch, the earth tilted beneath her and fell away and she was carried up into the storm.

2 RAIN

Misty rain blew in sheets across the dark, deserted car park, as the wind moaned and whistled through the open cattle sheds along its southern perimeter. Here and there, isolated street lights valiantly tried to shine through the drizzle, but merely succeeded in highlighting each new pulse of rain that blew into their lonely cones of light. With every gust, visibility was reduced to just a few tens of yards. In the distance the smudged grey suggestion of three approaching figures was lost to view as yet another veil of rain blew in. Once it had lashed through and moved on to rattle the battered metal fence panels of the cattle pens, the figures resolved into the form of three teenagers.

The three brothers looked sullen and bored as they meandered slowly across the expanse of tarmac that served on different days of the week as either a car park or a cattle market in the small market town of Liskeard. Their heads hung low and they dragged their feet through the puddles. Their rain soaked hair was plastered to their foreheads, the clumped, wet strands serving as conduits for little rivulets of icy water that ran across their faces, and down inside the collars of their jackets. One of the three tutted loudly and angrily swiped a stream of rainwater away with the back of his hand.

"I hate Christmas!" he said. "I don't know why we're even bothering to go out shopping, especially in this weather. It's not like we are going to find any decent presents in this town anyway!"

"That's because Liam didn't bother to sort anything out until the last minute," said Travis to Evan, the first of the brothers to have spoken, "as usual!"

"That's right," replied Liam, the target of Travis's last remark, "blame me again - you always do! This just happens to be the only day we've had when Mum and Dad haven't been around."

"Well you didn't have to wait until they went to the theatre," countered Travis. "You could have come into town on any day you wanted."

"Whatever," replied Liam, feigning disinterest. "But it's not my fault it's raining, it would've been raining no matter what day I had chosen!"

"True," agreed Evan, recognising that their shared irritation about the weather could be a good way of ending the developing argument before it really got started. "It does nothing but rain here, and there's nothing to do, just like the rest of Cornwall. I mean come on! We're only days away from Christmas, shouldn't it at least be snowing or something?"

Of the three brothers, Liam and Travis were the two most

inclined to disagree and argue. Even on those occasions where one was in agreement with the other, or was impressed with something the other had done, they were unlikely to ever admit to it. It wasn't that they disliked each other, in many ways they were very close, it was just that if any of the three were going to clash over anything, it was a good bet it would be Travis and Liam. There was no reason that was obvious to anyone else as to why this should be the case, but, it had always been that way, and Evan generally found himself left in the role of peacemaker.

Another gust of wind whistled in and thrummed around the metal sign that welcomed visitors to the car park in both English and Cornish. Icy rain lashed against the brothers' backs, and instinctively, they hunched their shoulders, attempting expose as little of their bodies as possible to the cold and wet.

"Come on you two," said Evan in defiance of the weather, "let's just get these last few presents bought, and then we can go home and get back to playing computer games."

Twisting ribbons of rain raced past, chasing one another across the surface of the car park and Liam, Evan and Travis reluctantly followed them in the direction of the town centre.

It was getting late in the day to be out shopping, and the weak winter sun, already obscured by a blanket of low grey rain clouds, had long since set, as the three teenagers walked dejectedly towards the main shopping street. Despite the grand facades of the many imposing buildings constructed during the copper mining boom of the 1800s, the town was quiet at the best of times, almost as if it never quite recovered from the decline that followed. On this particular day any other prospective shoppers had long since been driven back to their homes by the relentless rain. The occasional car hissing past along the wet road was pretty much all the company they had. The rain continued as they made their way through the town, blurring and streaking the Christmas lights that were strung across the roads and wound around the town's Christmas tree that stood by the fountain. Due to its location close to one the town's seating areas, and therefore one of the main hang-outs for the local youth, only the top two thirds of the tree were decorated. Over the years, this had proved to be a workable compromise between having no lights on the tree at all, and having to replace broken and missing bulbs on the lower limbs on a daily basis.

The brothers' moods did not improve as they half-heartedly drifted from one shop to another in search of Christmas presents for their family and friends. Eventually they reached the Christmas tree, its branches whipping back and forth in the wind as the suspended coloured lights bobbed and swung precariously below.

"Let's go down Fore Steet," suggested Travis, "It's the only road we haven't tried yet."

They crossed over the deserted main road, and headed down the steep hill past the town museum and clock tower until they reached the junction with Fore Street, a pedestrianised row of shops that headed back in the general direction of home, and which represented the final stage of their journey.

They rounded the corner and began to make their way past a little arcade of shops on their right. The first few shops were set back from the road, and separated from it by a covered walkway which was accessed via a series of archways. To reach any of the shops one had to first walk through one of the arches into the covered area, and the cross the walkway to the shop door. The brothers could have chosen to use the walkway and shelter from the rain for a few seconds, but they were so wet already it did not seem worth it.

When they were about halfway past the arcade, Travis suddenly stopped and looked behind him. "Wait, did you hear that?" he asked the other two.

"Hear what?" replied Liam.

"Footsteps," said Travis.

"Nope," said Liam, "there's no one around. It was probably just our footsteps you heard echoing through the arches."

"I don't think so, it sounded more like a child, you know like quick little steps."

"No one else would be stupid enough to be out in this weather," said Liam. "You're hearing things, there's no one there. Come on, let's just get finished and get home, I'm fed up with this."

Liam and Evan started walking along Fore Street again, and had almost reached the far end of the arcade when Evan noticed that Travis had not moved since they stopped.

"Come on Trav!" called Evan.

Travis did not react, and continued standing in the rain staring straight ahead.

"Travis!" Evan called again more loudly than last time.

"What?" said Travis looking around him in confusion for a moment, and then continued: "Oh, right, sorry, I was just thinking," before starting to walk forwards again to join his brothers.

"Well I hope it was about something good," replied Liam irritatedly, "cos we've got nothing better to do than stand around in the rain waiting for you."

"Stop moaning Liam," Travis said, "you're soaked through already, it isn't going to make you any wetter."

After a few more yards though, Travis had started to slow down again, and eventually stopped moving completely in front of a scruffy looking second-hand shop.

"Liam," called Evan smiling, nodding towards Travis, "have you seen this?"

Liam turned around to look at Travis, who was by now facing the window of the shop but gazing forward as if in a trance, even the cold rain running down inside the collar of his jacket didn't appear to be bothering him.

"Oi!" shouted Evan, "Wake up will you? What's the matter with you anyway?"

Travis blinked once or twice, and looked around him as if unsure for a moment of where he was.

"I'm not sure," replied Travis eventually, "I feel really weird though, it's like I almost fell asleep standing up. I remember thinking I heard footsteps, and the next thing I knew I was standing here. No wait, I was imagining how this street would look if it was snowing, but now, oh I don't know, it's gone now."

"Sounds like when we all got flu last year," said Evan. "I remember getting a bit delirious then. You've probably been out in the cold too long."

"Yeah, maybe," conceded Travis, who was now feeling a bit more like himself, and had found something to focus his attention on. "Hang on a second," he said to the others, looking into the window of the shop and craning his neck left and right trying to peer round the various stacked up items on display. "I just want to have a quick look in here before we go home."

"You won't find any magic gear in there!" said Liam dismissively. "It's just an old junk shop, and anyway you never practice your tricks anymore, so there's no point in looking, is there?"

"I'm not looking for magic stuff actually!" replied Travis, offended. "And for your information, I don't need to practice it all the time, you never forget it."

Travis had developed an interest in conjuring from quite a young age, but as he had grown older, and the opinions of his friends began to have more importance to him than those of his family, he had started to feel slightly uncomfortable and embarrassed about it. Now, despite still secretly harbouring an interest, he played it down to the point that the only people likely to mention it anymore were his brothers

"Well why don't you go in and look?" suggested Evan, "We can start walking home, and you can catch us up when you're finished."

"No, wait for me," said Travis, "I'll only be a couple of minutes."

Evan and Liam reluctantly turned around and squelched back towards the old shop, their sodden clothing coming into chilled and unwelcome contact with the skin of their legs as they walked. Evan stopped in the pool of yellow light on the wet flagstones outside the battered door to the shop, and pushed it open. A wave of warmth broke over them as the door swung inward, and quickly drained out into the cold night. The bell above the door dinged as they pushed through and stood dripping just inside. A trail of water drops, rapidly soaking into the worn wooden floorboards, led to Travis who was standing over at an old dresser in a far corner of the shop, rummaging through the various items piled up on its heavily laden shelves. Liam and Evan looked at each other. Liam rolled his eyes and shook his head, introducing the cold wet fabric of his soaking shirt collar to the back of his neck. It was going to be a long wait.

"I knew we should have carried on home," grumbled Evan. "It's not like it's far, he could have walked back on his own!"

By this time they were all feeling pretty fed up.

"I've just about had enough of this Christmas already," said Liam. "It's not like it used to be when we were little; it was so exciting, and we used to get fantastic presents. It kind of feels all dull and 'meh' nowadays."

"Come on Travis!" called Evan grumpily. "This Christmas is officially lame! Let's get out of here."

"You know, lads," began a new voice that had unexpectedly joined the conversation, causing the three to jump, "you really should be a little careful about what you say at this time of year."

Evan glanced at Liam and rolled his eyes again, carefully out of sight of the elderly shopkeeper whom they had now identified as the source of the voice, as if to say: "Here we go, more advice we don't need from adults!"

"And why would that be?" said Liam, a little more rudely than he intended. The shopkeeper seemed to realise that he hadn't meant to sound as disrespectful as he did, and carried on:

"You do know that tonight is the Winter Solstice don't you?" asked the shopkeeper with a note of concern in his voice.

"No," replied Evan, "why? What's the Winter Solstice?"

"It's the turning point of the year," said the old man. "The deepest part of winter, and the longest night of the year. Some people say that it's a time of increased supernatural activity. That's why you should be careful what you say. In our world, words are just words, but in the world of the supernatural, they could be a magic incantation or a binding contract. Who knows?"

Seeing that his customers were starting to feel a little uneasy, he changed his tone.

"But, if you think about it, if it's the longest night of the year, then obviously, from then on the days must start to lengthen again; so it's also the point when the light starts to return. That's why there have historically been so many celebrations and festivals at this time of year".

"You mean like Christmas?" said Liam.

"Well yes, but that's just one of the mid-winter celebrations, it goes back a lot further than what we now think of as Christmas," he said. "There have been festivals to mark the Winter Solstice for thousands of years. Actually, they say that the tradition of giving Christmas presents dates right back to the Roman festival of Saturnalia."

"Saturnalia?" queried Evan, the name sounded very close to that of the planet Saturn, and astronomy was a subject that was beginning to interest him more and more. "What was Saturnalia?"

"Well, as far as I know," began the shopkeeper, "it was a solstice celebration in Roman times. It was filled with the usual drunkenness and partying, but what made Saturnalia different was that it was a time when all the normal rules were reversed. The servants would become the masters, and the nobility would wait on their former subjects. The whole celebration was presided over by the Lord of Misrule, who would be responsible for ensuring that these rules were followed, and that everyone had a good time. But there were lots of other winter festivals throughout Northern Europe and Britain and they go back way beyond the Romans."

"Anyway," he continued, gesturing towards a wall of floor-to-ceiling bookshelves on one side of the shop, "I've got lots of books on the subject of midwinter rituals and celebrations. You should really take a look, you never know when you might need information like that."

The combination of the shopkeeper's serious tone, the atmosphere of the old junk shop, and the strange feeling he had experienced outside was making Travis feel quite uncomfortable. However, despite this, he soon resumed his searching at the back of the shop, while Evan walked over to the bookshelves for a closer look. "Well," he reasoned to himself, "you can't be too careful can you?" He quickly scanned the cliff face of books. They mostly appeared to be very old, bound in faded leather in dull reds, greens, and browns, and had titles like "Midwinter Rituals of Pagan Britain", "A Guide to the Winter Solstice.", and "The Winter Solstice For Dummies". There was even a very old battered academic-looking volume entitled "A Study of Ancient Solstice Magic."

Liam however, did not seem to be as worried about the man's warnings as his brothers and replied: "Well, thanks for the information, but I don't think we need to worry about anything supernatural happening in Liskeard. Nothing ever happens here."

At that moment, Travis emerged from the pile of objects he was rummaging through at the back of the shop. "Whoa!" he exclaimed, cradling a small silver object in his hands as he turned around. "This would make a great present!" He walked over to the counter, placed an ornate paper knife on its surface, and asked the shopkeeper: "How much is this please?"

"Ah, now that looks like something special. You, my friend, have a good eye!" said the shopkeeper, smiling at Travis.

"Really!" said Travis excitedly. "It looks pretty old. Do you know when was it made?"

"No idea," replied the shopkeeper smiling. "I don't think

I've ever seen it before, although that's nothing unusual in this shop, especially with my memory!"

Evan and Liam, with their interest now aroused by what the shopkeeper had just said, crowded around Travis at the counter, eager for a closer look at the paper knife. It appeared to be old, but still bright silver, with intricate carving on the handle that almost seemed to twist and coil around the handle as it caught the light. Travis picked up the knife again and examined it closely. On one side a design of interlocking snowflakes adorned the handle and flowed down onto the blade in a sinusoidal wave, occasionally casting little spiralling eddies off to one side or the other, the flakes gradually thinning out and reducing in number until they finally ran out about a third of the way down the blade. The metal on this side of the knife was highly polished, and the light flashed off it as Travis moved it around. He turned the knife over in his hand. The metal on the other side was finished differently; it was slightly dull, so that the blade itself looked as though it had been frozen, and when he angled it against the light, he could just make out the impossibly intricate meshing of frost ferns covering the whole of both the handle and the blade. Just like real frost ferns that he had seen on his morning paper-round covering the windows and bonnets of parked cars, these had been carved so that each fern was both distinct from its neighbours whilst at the same time flowing seamlessly into them.

"How much do you want for it?" asked Travis, pulling his last five pound note out of his wallet.

The shop keeper picked up the knife and examined it through a jeweller's loupe. "It really is quite lovely; excellent craftsmanship," he muttered to himself as he turned the knife backwards and forwards in front of his eyes.

Travis was beginning to worry that if the shopkeeper kept this up much longer he would decide he didn't want to sell it after all.

"Well," he declared, "it's certainly very old, and extremely well made. I don't know how they would have produced something of this quality back when it was made." Suddenly the old man seemed to make up his mind. He stood upright, and placed his jeweller's loupe back down on the counter with a click. "No," he said abruptly, and Travis's heart sank. The more the shopkeeper enthused about the knife, the more he had wanted it. "No," repeated the man, "I couldn't possibly let this go for anything less than five pounds."

Travis could not give the man his money quickly enough. The shopkeeper wrapped up the knife in tissue paper, and placed it in a brown paper bag.

"There you are!" he said. "Take care of it, and I hope it makes a good Christmas present."

The brothers thanked him and made their way out through the shop door and back into the wet Cornish night. Just as the door was closing, the shopkeeper called out to them:

"Turn the sign round on the door will you?" He looked down at his wristwatch and tapped the dial. "I think my watch is running slowly again. It's been doing it all afternoon, and I've lost count of the number of times I've had to reset it today. I thought the weather keeping everyone at home, but I expect that even without the rain they would have gone home ages ago. They probably didn't even think that the shop would still be open."

"No problem," said Travis, stepping back inside and flipping the cardboard sign in the door window round. From the outside it now read: "Closed - Gone to the Beach" Travis smiled at the irony and stepped outside into the cold winter rain again.

"Merry Christmas!" The shopkeeper called out. "And don't forget what I told you: be careful what you say around this time of year!"

"Merry Christmas!" they called back to him over the sound of the shop bell chiming as the door slammed shut on its spring.

"Come on," said Liam pulling his jacket tighter around him as the night air chilled his damp clothes again. "Let's get home, It feels like it's getting colder."

3 SNOW

After arriving back at their house, the brothers had dried themselves off and dressed in warm comfortable clothes. The only remaining outward sign of their journey through the rain was the pile of wet shoes and clothing that had been discarded in a sodden heap on the floor of the hallway in front of washing machine.

Liam, Evan and Travis laid out their meagre collection of recently purchased Christmas presents on the living-room floor. The few other gifts that they had managed to acquire in the preceding weeks were added to the small pile.

"Doesn't look like much does it?" said Liam despondently to no one in particular.

"Because it isn't much," replied Evan. "You really need to stop leaving everything to the last minute."

"Alright, don't you start as well. I thought moaning at me was supposed to be Travis's job."

Travis glanced over at Liam, but resisted the temptation to react to his comment.

Present wrapping was another job that none of them were particularly fond of, so Liam was surprised to find a feeling of mild excitement building inside him. He assumed that the mysterious assertions of the shop keeper in the second-hand shop were contributing to his mounting anticipation. The sound of the rain lashing against the living room windows with each new gust of wind, and the soft glow from the fairy lights wrapped around the garland draped across the mantelpiece added to the sensation. Whatever the cause, it felt very similar to how he used to feel as a child when Christmas was approaching.

"Why don't we put some carols on?" said Liam unexpectedly, "Dad's always going on about how it makes him feel Christmassy."

"What's got into you all of a sudden?" asked Travis.

"Yeah," added Evan with a smile, "Who are you and what have you done with Liam? You know, that moaning, grunting adolescent we've all come to know and love."

Despite his comments, Evan too had been feeling an increasing sense of anticipation and pulled his mobile phone from his pocket. He tapped and swiped at the touch screen for a few moments, and soon located a playlist of Christmas music online, which he began to broadcast through the phone's speaker. Soon they found themselves humming along to the familiar tunes that had not quite yet lost the power to transport them back to the Christmases of their childhoods. By now all three had begun to fully enter into the spirit of the occasion and were laughing, joking, and good naturedly jostling each other for the sticking tape and scissors.

"Oi Liam!" called Evan. "Pass the scissors over will you?"

The scissors had already changed hands a few times, and with this most recent interruption to his wrapping schedule, Liam turned and asked Travis: "Actually, can I borrow that letter opener you bought earlier? I bet it would do just as well as scissors for cutting this wrapping paper to size."

Travis took the paper knife out of its brown paper bag, unwrapped the layers of tissue paper that enveloped it, and passed it over.

"Ok," he said, "but be careful with it, I don't want it broken before it's even wrapped."

They then they returned to their wrapping activities once more. Liam found that if he folded the wrapping paper first and then ran his fingernail across the fold, the old paper knife would cut a perfectly straight line if he was careful. Slicing through the paper in this way was actually quite a satisfying experience, and he quickly became engrossed. Soon he had finished, and sat back contentedly to look at the intriguing, if modest, pile of presents that he had just wrapped, marvelling at just how different he now felt compared to his bad mood of earlier in the evening. The warm glow of excitement and anticipation that he was feeling was much more like how Christmas used to feel when he was younger. As far as Liam was concerned it was much more like how it ought to feel every year.

"You know," he said to both of his brothers at once, "It's weird, but I actually feel pretty excited about Christmas now."

"Yeah, me too," said Travis. "It's strange isn't it? I started to feel it when we were in that junk shop earlier. You don't think that's got anything to do with it do you? I mean after what that old guy was saying about mid-winter festivals and all that."

"Nah!" said Evan. "How could it? It's just because Christmas is getting close and we are all in here listening to carols in the warm away from the rain."

"Well actually that's another thing," said Travis.

"What's another thing?" asked Liam.

"The rain," replied Travis.

"What rain?" said Liam.

"Exactly!" continued his brother mysteriously. "I can't hear it any more, can you?"

Evan cocked his head to one side to listen. He could no longer hear the intermittent lashing of the raindrops against the window either. But what was more interesting still, was that the dark clouds just visible through the living room windows seemed to have taken on a curious yellowish-grey cast. The absence of the sound of rain hammering against the windows was only part of the story; now that they stopped to listen, it was actually unusually quiet, almost quiet enough for…

"You don't think…" began Evan, but the others were way ahead of him and were already on their feet heading for the window.

"Snow!" said Travis with an almost child-like joy arriving at the window first. "It's snowing, I don't believe it, it's Cornwall, and it's snowing!"

Travis quickly unlocked the back door and ran out into the garden, amazed at the covering of snow that had accumulated in the short time they had been in the house wrapping presents.

As he followed his brother out on to the snow covered patio just outside the back door, Liam realised that he still had hold of the paper knife, and he turned back to the house to put it safely on the coffee table until they returned. He didn't want to risk losing it outside so soon after Travis had bought it, he could just imagine Travis's reaction, he would never hear the end of it.

As he turned to take the paper-knife back inside, Liam found that as he gazed into the gently drifting flakes, they seemed to close in around him, softly cocooning him away from the rest of the world. Slightly mesmerised by the motion of the snow, he found it surprisingly easy to become fixated on a single snowflake. Strange, that. Amongst all the snow he was able to pick out an individual flake so easily. As he looked, it appeared to him whichever snowflake he focussed on was not falling like those around it, but danced around as if on the end of an invisible string, tugged by an unseen hand. As he concentrated on it, it seemed to dance further and further away from him luring him deeper into the strangely inviting tunnel of white. Even though in one part of his mind he was well aware that his feet were still on the ground, on some other level he felt as though he was drifting along with the snow, following the dancing flake into the tunnel. The temptation to mentally follow the snowflake was quite strong, and Liam would have done so had it not been for a soft tap that he felt against his back. He pushed the distraction to the back of his mind, and tried ignore it, but it happened again a little more forcefully than before. This time it was harder to ignore and his attention was drawn away. As he mentally withdrew, the entrancing snowflake followed him back. He found that very strange, and was considering investigating it a little more when a third much harder thud hit him on his shoulder, showering snow across the side of his face. Evan and Travis laughed at the direct hit they had scored with their third snowball. Liam smiled at the attack, and brushed the snow from his face. Still slightly disorientated, for a moment he was unsure that he had ever actually returned inside, but the paper knife was gone from his hand, so he scooped up a handful of snow from the patio, hurled it in the direction of his two brothers and ran out into the garden to rejoin them.

4 BLOOD

Travis's excitement at the unexpected snowfall was infectious, and soon the brothers were running around the garden laughing and hurling snowballs at each other, and occasionally at the windows of the house. One particularly well aimed shot hit Liam on the back of the head, and an icy sludge ran down inside his collar. However, this time it was nothing like as unpleasant as the cold water soaking through their clothes earlier in the town.

Liam bent down, picked up a generous handful of snow and began to mould it into perfect slushy retaliation.

After creating a few more snowballs he noticed that his hands were becoming less inclined to follow simple instructions from his brain as they began to numb from contact with the freezing snow.

"Hang on you two. Wait! Ceasefire!" he called out, "I need to put some gloves on, my hands are freezing." The response to this request was, of course, a well aimed

25

snowball from Evan that exploded across the side of his head. "Wait Evan!" he laughed shaking the snow from his face and hair, "I really need my gloves." Liam dropped his snowball to the ground and stuffed his hands into his coat pockets to retrieve his gloves. He immediately regretted it, as something sharp, cold and unexpected bit into his palm. He let out a yelp of pain.

He instinctively jerked his hand out of his pocket. Something wickedly sharp buried deep within his pocket had cut into the palm of his hand. Sucking in cold air through his gritted teeth and keeping the injured hand tightly balled up in a vain attempt to ease the pain, he carefully patted down the pocket from the outside with his other hand. Through the thick fabric of his coat it felt like there was nothing there, and so cautiously and awkwardly he slipped his uninjured hand deep inside the pocket. To his surprise he found it to be completely empty. His hand was starting to sting intensely now, and afraid of how bad the injury might be, he gingerly uncurled his fingers and looked down. A single drop of blood rolled down his palm and fell towards the newly fallen snow. As bright and red and round as a holly berry, the drop seemed to fall earthward in slow motion as the three teenagers looked on. For what felt like minutes they were captivated by the path of the drop of blood until its sudden impact with the snow snapped them back to reality. Although it cannot possibly have happened that way, they all felt as though the world held its breath as the drop fell, until, at the instant it touched the snow, it seemed as if there was a vast silent expulsion of air that tore away the clouds and shook the stars.

The snow sucked greedily at the drop of blood, and the perfect crimson circle rapidly spread out into, fading to pink as it expanded. In moments, fresh snow had covered the spot where it fell. The snowfall had not stopped in the time since the three of them had come out into the garden, and by now it was falling very heavily. The brothers looked at one another, suddenly not so sure that they wanted to be outside anymore.

"Whoa! Did you feel that?" asked Liam.

"Yeah, kind of," replied Evan.

"Kind of?" said Liam incredulously. "There is no 'kind of' about it, something definitely happened just then."

"Yeah, something happened alright, you cut yourself you pillock!" said Travis, trying to cover up his own unease.

"I mean apart from that!" replied Liam glancing around nervously.

Travis was about to respond when he became aware of the peculiar detached sensation that had gripped him outside the second hand shop starting to develop again. This time it made him feel much more uneasy. He looked from right to left, once again thinking that he could sense movement just beyond his field of vision.

"Guys," he called to his brothers, but before he was able to finish the thought, he thought he caught the sound of distant laughter, barely audible over his voice.

"What?" replied Evan.

"Did you hear something?"

"Hear what?" said Evan. "Wait, is this like the footsteps you heard in Fore street again?"

"Dunno, maybe," replied Travis, "I do feel a bit weird, yeah, you're right, it was probably nothing."

Now that he had a little time to think, his concerns did seem a bit silly. The laughter he thought he had heard had probably been exactly that. After all, it was very likely that were that they weren't the only people outside enjoying the snow.

"Well, whatever it was," said Liam, I don't like it. I'm going back inside. Right now."

"Yeah," agreed Travis with audible relief that someone other than himself was feeling uncomfortable with the current situation. "Besides, you probably ought to clean that cut up."

Returning to the house, the brothers were confronted by the sight of the back door standing open, a small pile of snow had accumulated on the carpet inside the door.

"Liam!" said Travis accusingly.

"What?" replied Liam.

"What do you think?" Travis continued. "You left the door open; it's going to be freezing cold inside now!"

"It wasn't me," stated Liam.

"Yeah, that's right, it wasn't you," said Travis sarcastically, "not even when you went back to put my letter opener down."

"Alright," replied Liam. "Shut up moaning, and stop making such a fuss, it'll soon warm up again," adding: "Mum" as a final barb.

To drive home his point, Liam entered the house last, making a show of closing the door behind him, and even the deafening crash that usually accompanied this activity was quickly muffled by the snow that continued to smother the world beyond the back door.

Outside the snow was still falling so quickly that soon it had completely covered the antique silver paper knife that had fallen from Liam's pocket when he snatched his hand out in pain just a few minutes earlier.

5 DISTURBANCE

Back inside the house, Liam set to work cleaning up the cut on his hand. To his relief, the incision appeared to be surgically clean; he had not been looking forward to the pain that would have accompanied removing any debris from the wound. A short search through the kitchen cupboards, revealed an ancient looking bottle of antiseptic solution in the first aid box. After soaking a piece of gauze that was grubby with age in the liquid, he cautiously applied it to the palm of his hand. As he had expected, the soothing coolness of the solution quickly transformed into the familiar burning he remembered from when his mother used to have to administer similar treatments to the three of them in years past. And, as it used to do in those far off days of childhood, the sensation increased to an almost unbearable intensity, before rapidly easing again. Liam sucked air in through clenched teeth, and shook his hand from side to side until the stinging passed.

Even though they were back within the warm cocoon of their house, and Liam had attended to his injury, the brothers could not quite shake off the feeling of unease that they had felt in the garden. Sitting in the living room, surrounded by the familiar sights and sounds of home, things somehow still did not feel quite right. The heavy snowfall outside continued, and seemed to have transported them from the typical damp Cornish evening of earlier to deepest winter in mere hours.

The odd feeling that something fundamental about the world had changed continued to concern Liam. Eventually, as a way of putting his mind at rest, he summoned up the courage to investigate and ventured to the back door. Slipping between the drawn curtains that separated the sitting room from the window bay he approached the double doors that led to the garden. The comparative darkness of the curtained off area gave him a sense of separation from both the house and the garden. A thrill of excitement ran down his spine as he felt both vulnerable at being away from the warmth and light of the sitting room whilst still being in the safety of the house. Looking through the windows he could see that the snow was still falling steadily, but other than that there was no indication that anything unusual was happening. Reassured, he pressed down the handle, pushed the door open a little, and poked his head outside. As soon as he did so, he found himself gasping for breath as the air was sucked from his lungs by the sudden drop in temperature. The world beyond was white, silent, and cold and there was not the slightest breeze, as if the sheer weight of falling snow had blocked out the wind. Liam quickly jerked his head back inside and slammed the door closed.

"Bloody Hell!" he gasped as he leaned back against the door breathing heavily.

"What?" said Evan, drawing the curtains wide as both he and Travis barged into the bay and joined Liam at the double doors. Evan opened the door again, and they were both similarly startled by the dramatic change in the world outside.

They gazed around, gradually processing the scene before them. The snow was now falling so thickly that they could not see the summer house at the end of the garden. In fact they were unable to judge how far they could see at all, as the falling snow obscured every landmark that they looked for in the garden. Familiar everyday sounds were smothered. Even the ubiquitous noise of cars driving along the nearby roads, until recently so familiar that it was barely noticeable, was gone, no doubt due to a combination of the roads now being impassable, and the sound-deadening effects of the snow. The everyday world they knew seemed to have drawn away and surrendered to the deepening winter. All this generated a strange sense of isolation that made the brothers feel uneasy and jumpy.

As they gazed around, Travis's eye was suddenly drawn by an unexpected impression of movement off to his left, that he felt more than saw. Oddly panicked, he jerked his head around, unreasonably afraid of what might be there, but as soon as he glanced towards it, it was gone.
Evan noticed Travis's sudden movement.

"What? What is it?" he said, struggling to keep the note of panic out of his voice.

"It's nothing," replied Travis. "I thought I saw something move, but it's nothing."

"Something like what?" asked Liam, surprised at the urgency, and the quavering he heard in his own voice.

"I thought it was like a flicker of movement or something

over there," Travis said, nodding his head to the left, "but it wasn't, there's nothing there."

"Probably just the snow playing tricks on your eyes," said Evan, as much to reassure himself as the others. "You can't see anything through this!"

The light spilling from the back door was illuminating every swirling snowflake, and hemming the world in around them, making it impossible to make out anything at all in the garden beyond. To Evan it felt like they were trapped within a snow globe. The random drifting of the illuminated snowflakes seemed to throw the world, or at least that little part of it that they could see, into a disorientating, erratic motion and a sudden sensation of dizziness gripped him, threatening to throw him off balance. He reached for the door frame with his hand. The reassuring solidity he felt under his fingers helped to calm him down again.

"Yeah," added Liam, "Evan's right. You probably just picked up on the movement of the snowflakes in your peripheral vision." The application of logic seemed to do the trick. Feeling reassured, they closed the door and returned to the warmth and light of the front room, and after a few more minutes, Liam had quite forgotten that at exactly the same time as Travis had jerked his head around, his own eyes had also been drawn in the same direction.

The next few hours passed normally enough, and although the occasional distant wailing noise filtered through into the house, it was quickly dismissed as probably the siren of a police car on its way to assist a stranded motorist. The brothers all conveniently forgetting that when they were outside, sound didn't seem to travel any distance at all.

"How about a film?" suggested Liam. The unspoken idea

being that a familiar Christmas film would help them forget the strangeness they all experienced in the garden earlier.

"Good idea!" said Evan "What about 'Home Alone'? That's a Christmas film."

"No thanks!" retorted Liam. "I can't stand that film. Let's watch a Harry Potter film. They always make me feel Christmassy."

"OK," said Evan. "The Philosopher's Stone then, that's got a Christmas scene in it."

"It's a pretty long film," said Liam, "about three hours or so isn't it? What time is it now?"

Evan pressed the button on the front of his phone, and the screen illuminated on command.

"That's weird. It's only just after six, we've got ages," he said. "But it feels loads later than that to me. It seems like hours ago that Liam cut himself."

"What?" said Travis. "Only six? That can't be right. I thought it was at least eleven, possibly even midnight by now."

"Well, my phone's never been wrong before," responded Evan. "It even adjusted itself automatically when the clocks went back, so there's no reason to doubt it."

"Well don't moan about it," said Liam. "We've got loads of time. Mum and Dad won't be back from the theatre until about midnight, and anyway, it doesn't matter how late we stay up: it's Christmas."

Sometime later the brothers were slouching on the settees in the sitting room engrossed in the film and eating microwave popcorn that Evan had found in one of the kitchen cupboards. They were all starting to feel a little dozy when suddenly the calm atmosphere was disturbed by a hollow rattling that seemed to originate from just outside the back door. Liam, who was sitting closest, jumped up and ran over to the window. Quickly pulling back the curtains he looked outside. As far as he could see, which due to the falling snow was not very far, everything appeared normal.

"Probably just a cat trying to get into the bin," said Liam, once the initial shock had passed. "It'll have run off by now."

They listened intently for a few more minutes, but when nothing more was heard, they returned to watching their film. The story had progressed to the scene where Harry opened the jumper that Ron's mother had knitted for him as a Christmas present, when they once again heard a soft clattering coming from the vicinity of the rubbish bin. Having established earlier that the noise was probably being made by cats, Travis picked up a cushion and threw it at the window.

"Bugger off!" he shouted.

Liam and Evan sniggered briefly in appreciation of Travis's advanced grasp of the English language and comic timing and they returned to the film.

The next time it happened, the noise was much louder. A sudden crash rattled the windows, and instantly the camaraderie and contentment of a few moments ago were gone. Evan looked at Travis, with fear widened eyes. He could see his expression reflected in Travis's face and knew that that his brother was similarly concerned by these developments.

Suddenly, Liam jumped up from where he was lying along one of the settees: "Bloody cats!" he shouted in an attempt to cover up the fear that was building within him, and ran for the back door, propelled by a surge of pure adrenalin.

"Hang on Liam!" called Evan. "It could be anything!"

"Or it could just be a cat," said Liam, opening the door and stepping outside without even allowing himself time to think. Evan and Travis quickly followed him out battling inner conflicts between the need for self preservation and the fraternal instinct to protect one of their own. Once he was back out in the garden again some of Liam's bravado left him and he waited for his brothers to catch up before slowly advancing round the corner to the partially covered porch way where the dustbin was kept. The closer they got the more the tension mounted as their imaginations started playing tricks on them in the short distance they had to travel to reach the porch. Steeling himself against what he knew was, or at least desperately hoped to be, fear of his own making, Liam leapt around the corner.

Before him was a perfectly ordinary upturned rubbish bin.

"There you are, I told you," said Liam trying hard to keep the relief from his voice. "Cats!"

A depression in the snow beside the bin seemed to indicate where the unfortunate animal had landed, and next to that a small patch of snow had been stained purple. Liam quickly glanced around for the piece of tissue paper that had no doubt fallen from the bin and leached its lurid dye out into the damp snow, as he reached down and stood the rubbish bin back upright. Evan, meanwhile, took a closer look at the paw prints surrounding it. He followed the tracks into the garden with his eyes for as far as he was able to until they disappeared from view in the whiteout. Smiling to himself, he recalled the image of cat tearing off into the garden in a state of high feline embarrassment, with its tail arched high in the air behind it and its hind legs almost overtaking its fore legs in its haste to escape.

"Hang on a second," he said to himself with a little shock, "that never happened, did it?"

He blinked in confusion as he tried to reconcile the indisputable fact that they had heard the cat from inside the house with the curtains closed with the startlingly clear memory he seemed to have of witnessing it racing off into the snow. However before he could spend too much time contemplating it, sounds of activity filtered into his mind as Travis and Liam began the unpleasant task of returning the spilt rubbish to the bin, and the peculiar sensation soon passed.

"Come on Evan!" said Travis. "We could do with a hand here!"

"What?" said Evan distractedly. "Oh yes, just a sec."

"Not in a sec," said Travis, his breath forming clouds around his head in the cold still air. "We need some help now, it's bloody freezing!"

"Alright," said Evan with an irritated tone in his voice.

Something about those animal tracks didn't quite add up, but he was finding it hard to focus on exactly what it was about them that was bothering him. Each time he tried to concentrate, his mind drifted off on to other things, mostly the patterns in the swirling snow. Evan shook his head and snapped back into alertness, frustrated at how his mind was acting like a saboteur, gradually introducing progressively more and more vague and dreamlike thoughts until he caught himself just standing staring into space. The maddening swirling of the flakes wasn't helping either, how he was supposed to concentrate, he thought, with all this snow spiralling around was anybody's guess. Oddly he noticed that the more he followed the spirals around, the slower they seemed to spin, whilst at the same time the rest of the world seemed to start to rotate in the opposite direction. "Oh, for crying out loud!" He muttered as he realised that it had just happened again.

"What?" said Travis.

"'What', what?" replied Evan, then added: "Oh, nothing," as he realised that Travis must have heard him.

Evan turned to help his brothers, immediately forgetting what had been on his mind. When all of the rubbish had been placed back in the bin, they returned to the house and locked the door behind them.

"Told you there was nothing to worry about," said Liam.

But Evan wasn't listening: now he was inside, and out of the swirling, confusing snow, he realised what it was that had been concerning him. Even though the tracks in the garden had been small enough to be a cat, he could not recall the last time he had seen one wearing shoes.

"Umm," said Evan, struggling to find a way to voice what he wanted to tell Liam and Travis without having to endure a barrage of ridicule.

"What?" said Travis.

"Well," replied Evan, "it's just, well you know those paw prints around the bin outside?"

"Yes," said Liam.

"While we were outside something about them seemed odd, but I couldn't put my finger on what it was."

"And?" prompted Travis, as he waited for Evan to continue.

"And, I've just remembered."

"Well, go on then, what was it?" said Liam.

"To be honest," answered Evan, "it's probably easier if I just show you."

6 LOST

Evan and Liam stood up and prepared to go out to investigate the paw prints.

"Hang on a second," Travis called out and he quickly detoured over to the coffee table, and hunted around for the letter opener. The other two looked at him quizzically.

"What?" he said to their unasked question. "I just wanted to take the paper knife, you can't be too careful, can you? Anyway, I can't find it. You'd better not have lost it Liam!"

"Alright, calm down," retorted Liam, "It'll be here somewhere, surely you remember me bringing it back in, you made enough fuss about the door being left open!"

"Stop bickering you two!" Interjected Evan, "Seriously! It gets a bit boring after a while! Now come on, there's something I want to show you."

Travis joined Evan and Liam at the back door. He pressed

down on the handle and pushed it open. Despite the fact that none of them had noticed, evidently the wind had picked up since the dead calm of earlier, and he found himself having to strain his arm muscles against the pull of the door as the breeze threatened to fling it open. Forcing the door closed behind them against the wind, the three of them returned to the garden and started to make their way round to the porch that housed the rubbish bin. Even though it was only a short distance away, the snow was falling much faster now, and was being whipped around by the wind, making it difficult for them to see where they were going. Holding up one arm in front of his face to try and keep out the driving snow, Evan led the way back to the porch. When he arrived, he was disappointed to find that the footprints they had come to investigate had by now been reduced to little more than indistinct depressions in the snow.

"Well that's that then," said Travis. "You'll have to tell us what you saw to us after all."

Evan sighed, and was trying to think how he was going to phrase it when an idea struck him: the tracks that led off into the garden were the most recent, perhaps they were still clear enough to see.

"No," he said. "I think I can still show you, follow me." Evan stepped down from the porch and led his brothers along the path and into the blizzard that the garden had become. He turned to them to explain, but by now the wind had picked up so much that he was surprised to find that he had to raise his voice in order to be heard.

"The trail of footprints led off into the garden," he shouted, "so these will be the freshest tracks. They were only made after whatever-it-was knocked over the bin and ran off.

They might still be clear enough to make out." However, they soon discovered that the wind-blown snow had drifted over any evidence entirely.

"Ok, forget it, we're too late." Evan shouted above the wind.

"And?" said Travis.

"And what?" replied Evan.

"Well you dragged us out here to show us something, you clearly didn't think that just telling us would suffice, so what was it that you saw?"

"Oh yeah," began Evan, "Well, the tracks in the snow, I don't think they weren't paw prints, they looked more like footprints to me."

"And you couldn't just tell us that because?"

"I don't know really," began Evan, "at first, I just couldn't think straight, and then I thought you wouldn't believe me."

"And now you've dragged us all out here into the garden when there could be an intruder around?" said Liam angrily.

"I don't think it's anyone to be frightened of," replied Evan. "The footprints, they were really small like a child's, or maybe even smaller. But to be honest, I'm not sure I'm remembering anything properly at the moment, ever since it started snowing my mind seems to have been all over the place. It's got me a bit worried really. I wanted to be sure one way or the other whether it was footprints or paw prints, but I didn't want to have to come out here on my own."

"Well, if it was a kid, they probably just climbed over the wall from the park, they'll be gone again by now. Come on, we may as well go back inside." said Liam.

Evan turned around to head back to the house, but with a little jolt of fear he realised that even though they had only advanced a short way into the garden, they were no longer able see the house through the swirling snowflakes. Without warning, a wave of panic threatened to overwhelm him.

"OK, just calm down," he told himself. "It's not like the house has gone anywhere, you just can't see it. It's only a few feet away."

The three brothers turned around and Evan made his way to the front of the line once more. They had just started to walk back in the direction of the house, when Travis called out from the back of the line.

"Hey, you two, wait up a second!"

"What for?" called out Evan.

"Shhh!" retorted Travis urgently. "I thought I heard something."

They stopped and listened hard. If there had been a sound, they could not hear anything now above the howling wind. After a few seconds Travis decided that he must have imagined it, and was about to start walking back towards the house when he again thought he heard a noise carried on the wind.

"There it was again!" he shouted above the wind to the others. "Did you hear it that time?"

"Nope." said Liam. "I can't hear anything in this wind. You must be hearing things again. Come on, let's get going."

Then, Evan cocked his head to one side, thinking that he too had just caught a snatch of something that sounded out of place but then it too was torn away on the wind and lost.

"No, wait!" he said, "I think I heard something too!"

Travis called out once more from the back of the line.

"I can hear it better now," he said. "It sounds like a woman's voice! Come on!"

He turned the opposite way to their direction of travel, and immediately disappeared into the wall of swirling snow that obscured the end of the garden. Evan and Liam hurried to follow, and soon they were all plunging blindly through the night. Evan was beginning to feel that he was running faster than he felt was safe, when suddenly he thudded into the back of Travis, who had abruptly stopped moving.

"Ow! Travis!" he said just before the wind was knocked out of him by Liam careening in turn into his back. "You could've said you were going to stop!"

"Shh!" said Travis urgently. "I can't hear her anymore. I thought I was getting close but then her voice suddenly stopped!"

Liam listened hard, and then called out "This way," and ran off ahead of his brothers into the snow again. This time all three of them were able to hear the, by now, obviously distressed, cries coming from over by the fence that ran along the left-hand boundary of the garden. Almost immediately the sound faded away again, as if the woman was moving away from them at a pace much faster than the three of them could run. Then, as suddenly as they had started, the woman's cries stopped again, and the three teenagers came to a halt.

"Where is she?" asked Liam, his concern for the mysterious woman's welfare obvious from the tone of his voice. "Hello!" he shouted. "Where are you? We're coming to help you!" but his calls went unanswered. Gradually, a look of confusion crossed Evan's face.

"Um, I don't want to alarm anyone," he said, "but shouldn't we have run into the garden fence by now?"

"Yeah," said Liam. "That is strange," realising that they seemed to been chasing after the voice for a rather greater distance than their back garden actually extended.

"No," said Travis, "we must have got turned around in the snow. I mean we can barely see our hands in front of our faces in this."

"Yeah," replied Liam, "that must be it."

"And which way is it back to the house?" said Evan, struggling to keep his voice level. All of a sudden the strange feelings from earlier washed back over him like a cold Atlantic wave.

"Seriously!" he said, clearly panicked when no one offered a suggestion. "Where is the house? I want to go back inside."

"It's Ok," said Liam reassuringly. "Calm down a bit and think about it. The garden isn't that big, and it's rectangular. If we walk in a straight line for more than about fifteen paces we are bound to reach either the shed at the end of the garden, one of the side fences, or the house."

This seemed to have the desired effect, and Evan felt himself calm down a little.

"Yeah," he said. "That's true. I mean technically, we'd fall off the retaining wall that Dad never quite finished building, and probably break a leg before we walked into the shed. But yes, you're right. I was just getting freaked out."

"Ok then," said Liam, picking a direction at random, "we'll go this way." The three brothers headed off again into the snow, with Liam counting out each pace as they walked into the white-out again.

"1, 2, 3, 4, 5," he counted as they walked. In any direction they could see no further than about one arm's span away, so it was really no surprise that they had lost their bearings in a space as small as their own back garden. Just then Travis lost his footing, and slid a few feet past Liam before managing to stop himself again. "Careful!" laughed Liam. "You'll make us lose count."

"Alright," replied Travis. "I couldn't help it. The ground is really steep; our garden isn't this steep is it?"

"It probably just feels steep because it's so slippery," said Liam. "The garden does run down the hill quite a bit." Travis did not feel convinced, but no other explanation presented itself, and Liam sounded pretty sure of himself, so he let it go.

"6, 7, 8," Liam continued. He was starting to move a little more slowly now that he felt they were closing in on one boundary of the garden or another.

"9, 10, 11, 12, Ok," Liam called back from the front of the line. "We'd better slow it down now, we've been walking a little way, so we must be either heading for the house, or we are about to fall off the wall in front of the shed."

"13, 14, 15,"

"16,"

"Err," said Travis, "shouldn't we have hit something by now?"

"It was only an estimate," said Liam, "and anyway we may not have been walking exactly in a straight line."

"17, 18, 19,"

"Hang on!" said Evan. "Something's not right he..." but before he could finish voicing his thought, the woman's voice returned again.

"Help me!"

The voice was so close to Travis's right hand side that he spun round in shock, but still there was nothing to see. Suddenly the voice called out again, but this time from the other side.

"Please! Somebody help me!"

The brothers were terrified now and were spinning around on the spot trying to see where the woman's voice was coming from, when suddenly a shape materialised out of the snow immediately in front of them and collided with the group so hard that they were all sent sprawling on to the snow covered ground.

7 CELYN

Evan was the first of the brothers to recover from the collision. He staggered to his feet and looked around in a daze. Locating Travis and Liam where they lay half buried in the snow, he helped them each to their feet in turn.

"What on earth was that?" asked Travis, brushing the snow from his clothes.

"I think you'll find that it was her," said Evan, pointing to an area of ground behind the other two.

Travis and Liam turned and followed Evan's outstretched arm, to where a young woman lay sprawled out motionless on the snow. She had skin as white as the snow on which she lay, and her face was framed with long dark hair that was held in place by a thin circlet of white metal studded with dazzling gemstones as red as blood. Her clothing looked very old fashioned and ornate, almost as if she had just walked straight out of a fairy tale. She was certainly not the type of woman that any of them were used to seeing around Liskeard. All three of them stood transfixed, staring at what they each had independently decided must be the most beautiful creature they had ever seen. They were so captivated by the woman that none of them reacted when she began to move. Moaning, she raised her hand to her head and rubbed at her temple, then winced at the pain that she instantly felt. Suddenly her eyes flicked open, and she looked around wildly, obviously terrified of something. When she noticed the teenagers she tried to jump up to run away, but the action obviously set her head spinning and she fell back to the ground with an undignified thud and ended up sitting in the snow.

"It's OK. It's OK," said Evan, holding his hands out in front of him to show that they meant her no harm.

"Yes," said Liam. "We came to help you."

The woman looked at each of them in turn, and then said: "Well, if you really do want to help me, you can start by helping me up off the ground!"

For a few moments none of them reacted, they just stared at her dumbfounded by her beauty, and entranced by the sound of her voice, which seemed to have the power to deprive the listener of the ability to think of anything else at all. Unfortunately, although her voice seemed to be the only thing of any interest in the world to the three brothers, it also had the effect of lulling them into a trancelike state, and they did not really comprehend any of what she had just said.

"Seriously?" she said, clearly becoming irritated. "Are you just going to stand there like idiots, and leave me down here in the snow?"

This seemed to snap Liam out of his trance, and he held out his good hand to her. The woman reached up to his outstretched hand, closed her fingers around his and began to pull herself to her feet. The touch of her skin was unlike anything he had ever known, soft, warm and gentle, whilst at the same time sending little electric shocks through his brain. The sensation made him dizzy and he almost let her go again, but eventually he succeeded in pulling her to her feet.

"Well, finally!" said the woman as she stood indignantly in the garden, swatting and patting irritatedly at the snow that clung to her long heavy velvet skirt. The brothers hadn't moved, and Liam in particular was still reeling from the odd feelings that had coursed through him as he had helped the mysterious woman to her feet.

"Dullards!" she exclaimed. "I thought you said you were going to help me. Do you have any idea who I am?"

Evan was the first to react: "Well, er, actually, no," he said.

The sound of his own voice seemed to help him focus a little more. Something about the way this strange woman was reacting was starting to seem a little unfair to him. They were in their own back garden after all, and she was acting like she owned the place.

"And anyway we came chasing out here to help you, in the heaviest snow we've had in years I might add," he continued, starting to feel more and more annoyed at the injustice of the situation. "So you might try and show a bit of gratitude." Evan's minor outburst had caused Travis and Liam to shake off some of the vagueness that seemed to have affected them, and they both stared at Evan in shock. This had the potential to end badly. Evan glanced at their open-mouthed expressions and then back at the woman and suddenly felt guilty about how he had reacted, and added, "Ma'am." Somehow it seemed appropriate.

Since they had helped her to her feet, the woman's initial terror had disappeared, and she now seemed to radiate an odd kind of authority that was very difficult to resist.

"So, you really don't know who I am then? Well, perhaps you could do with a little reminder!" she said, turning her full attention on Evan. As she focussed on him, Evan's head began to swim, and the woman seemed to waver and shimmer in his vision. Little pin-pricks of bright white light sparked into life in his field of vision. Evan's thoughts became very sluggish and confused, and the ground seemed to tilt beneath his feet. He stumbled a couple of steps to the side, and shook his head to try and clear it. This seemed to have some of the desired effect and he was able to concentrate enough to notice that the woman was now staring quite intently at him.

"Show me your ears," she said suddenly.

"What?" said Evan. Clearly he was still confused; nothing she was saying seemed to make any sense at all to him.

"Pull back your hair," she commanded, "and show me your ears."

Before he even had time to think about the odd request, Evan found himself complying with the woman's instructions. She moved in close and examined his ears. A tingling sensation coursed across Evan's head as her strange perfume enveloped him, flowing into his lungs and sending his head spinning once more. He began to drift into a trance-like state, when the sound of her voice penetrated the haze in his mind.

"Wait," she said. "You three, you're not humans are you?"

The strange question, and especially the odd emphasis the she put on the word 'humans' caused the brothers to look at each other in confusion.

"What?" said Travis. "Are we what? Are we human? Of course we're flaming human! What do you think we are?"

"Well, now that," replied the woman in a considerably more friendly tone, "is rather interesting."

"Rather interesting?" queried Travis. "Why on earth would it be rather interesting that we are human?"

Independently, all three brothers realised that they were finding it much easier to think now.

"It's interesting to me," said the woman, "because I, and this may come as a surprise to you I'll wager, am not human. Your kind and mine don't often mix."

"Your kind?" said Travis. "You look pretty human to me."

"Well, looks can be deceiving, and that apparently works both ways. Now that I know what you are, it is entirely possible that you aren't as dim-witted as at first you seemed," said the woman with a smile. "My kind have the ability to exert our influence over those around us, but it does seem to have a particularly potent effect on humans. We can control it, but it takes a bit of effort, and obviously we have to know that we are dealing with humans in the first place."

"Ok," said Travis, "so let's say that you aren't human, what should we call you?" He then added as an afterthought: "I'm Travis, these two are Evan and Liam, my brothers."

"Well, it's nice to make your acquaintance Travis, Evan, and Liam," the woman replied turning to each one of them in turn. "My name is Celyn, and through the centuries, your race has tended to refer to mine as fairies."

"What?" spat Travis incredulously. "A fairy! I'm sorry Celyn, we may be human, but we're not children! You can't honestly expect us to believe that!" Now that he had finished speaking, Travis noticed that the wind strength had picked up even more, and it was starting to blow hard enough to cause all of the teenagers to take notice, even with the current distractions. Within seconds they were forced to hold their hands up over their faces to protect their eyes from the snow that was now being driven into them. But stranger than the sudden storm force winds was the reaction that it induced in the new arrival in the garden. Celyn's demeanour had changed, from one of assured authority, to fear, in seconds. She looked rapidly from right to left, and her eyes were open wide in terror.

"The storm is coming!" she cried in alarm. "We've got to get away from here quickly!"

"Whoa, alright, calm down," said Evan. "It's only a squall."

"Yes, thank you human boy," replied Celyn, a rising note of irritation adding to the fear in her voice. "I know what it is, and probably rather better than you do!"

"Actually," replied Evan affronted, "I'd rather you didn't call me 'boy' I'm fifteen years old, and we humans," he emphasised the word sarcastically, "tend to prefer..." but he stopped short. He tipped his head to one side, listening. Carried on the last gust of wind Evan thought he had heard the distant sound of dogs baying and yelping. It had sounded a long way off, but considering the unearthly silence that had accompanied the start of the snowfall, any distant sound at all would have seemed out of place. But now that the wind was truly howling and the driving snow was freezing his ears, he couldn't be sure, and decided that it was probably nothing after all. He was about to try and continue his discussion with the strange woman when he heard the sound again. This time it was much louder, and it definitely sounded like a pack of dogs, but why, he wondered, would a pack of dogs be running wild through a snowstorm in Liskeard? Even odder was the fact that he thought he could hear horses whinnying and men's voices calling out. He looked to his brothers, by the expressions on their faces it was evident that they too could hear the same sounds. By now, Celyn was clearly becoming very anxious.

"It's the Wild Hunt!" she said in a panicked voice. "We have to get out of the storm now!"

8 PURSUED

"What?" shouted Evan above the shrieking wind. "The Wild Hunt? What in the world is that?"

"Nothing," Celyn shouted back, "nothing of this world anyway. There's no time to explain. If you value your human lives, we need to run. Now!" And with that she gathered up armfuls of her long skirt and started to run into the storm. She was almost lost to sight in the whirling snow when Travis called out, urgently enough to stop her in her tracks.

"Celyn, wait! Our house is close by."

"Inside?" She shouted against the wind. "Yes, yes, inside; they won't be able to get to us if we are inside."

"But we don't know which way to go," Travis called back. "We can't find our way back through the snow!" The last of his words were torn away by the wind, as the storm's intensity rose to almost unbearable levels. In addition to the storm's increasing violence, the sound of the hunt was also getting louder. Celyn and the three brothers turned around in panic as the sound of the hunt seemed to come from all around them. From one side of the group would come the sound of snapping jaws and the howling of dogs, and then from the opposite side the pounding of thundering hooves. Disorientated, they felt as if they were in the centre of a mad whirlpool of sound. They didn't know which way to turn, and all the while, their faces were being stung by the wind-whipped snow. Panicked by the terrifying noises whirling around them, and effectively blinded by the walls of snow that closed in on the from all sides, the group staggered forward through the maelstrom in an attempt to flee. As they ran, Liam was battered into the centre of the group by something large and irresistibly strong. He did not get a clear look at it because of the driving snow, but was left with the impression of tense muscle covered with a layer of sweat-streaked brown hair. The mad snorting that accompanied it convinced him that he had just been side-swiped by the flank of a monstrous horse galloping past. He was thankful for the fact that he had not been trampled beneath its hooves. He just managed to stay on his feet, but was then knocked sideways again when Evan was similarly barged into the group from the other side. The otherworldly shouting of what they assumed were the riders of the horses continued to rotate wildly around them, making the group dizzy as they snapped their heads first one way then the other in an attempt to keep track of their pursuers. A sudden vicious snarling a few feet to Travis's right caused him to jump back towards the rest of the group, just in time to snatch the impression of a pair of madly snapping jaws, tearing into thin air where his leg had been an instant before. A moment later, the snarling was replaced with a pained yelping as the creature jerked back into the storm once more. Disorientated by the way that their tormentors seemed to swirl around them at speeds that no earthly creatures could hope to equal, the group plunged blindly forward into the storm again. Evan took the lead until Travis grabbed the hood of his jacket causing him to pull up suddenly just in time to prevent his head coming into contact with a pair of razor-sharp hooves that sliced through the air just in front of him.

As they ran on in panic the ferocity of the storm increased until, almost inevitably, a jagged bolt of lightning spat through the air on their left, illuminating the world around them for one terrifying instant. The light was so intense that it seared its way through the wall of snow that enclosed them and their world expanded alarmingly. For a split second, silhouetted against the light and shockingly close, they saw the hunt for the first time: Row after row of horses each frozen in a different phase of its gallop; innumerable hounds running flat out, streamlined and deadly with their ears flattened against their heads; and then there were the riders. Against the background of a sky bleached a pale violet by the flash, they too were frozen in place, some leaned forward over the necks of their mounts, instinctively reducing the surface they exposed to the wind. Others had their heads thrown backwards in ecstasy having fully given themselves over to the thrill of the hunt. At least one of them was riding side-saddle, her long tangled hair whipping around her face. Those who weren't between the group and the flash could be seen in more detail. Tattered strips of clothing flapped and snapped behind them like ancient flags ruined by the wind. Others were brandishing swords; burnt and corroded by a thousand lightning strikes, and all the more fearful because of their condition, as despite their wishes, each member of the group imagined the damage the burned jagged edges would do as they ripped through soft flesh.

In a fraction of a second, the light was gone, and they were instantly transported back to the small illusion of safety afforded by their cocoon of snow. But the horrifying afterimage of the hunt persisted for a few seconds more, drifting in front of their eyes in unnatural colours taunting and disorientating them.

Oddly, given the hopeless situation they found themselves in, Travis's mind had become strangely calm, as if this was all happening to someone else. The situation, however terrifying and bizarre was real, and panic could serve no more purpose. He found he was able to think very clearly, and a simple but previously elusive truth became apparent to him.

Turning to the rest of the group he screamed above the howling wind: "Uphill!"

"What?" shouted Evan back to him. "Why uphill?"

"Because when I slipped earlier, we were going downhill." replied Travis. ""The house is uphill!"

Instinctively they turned to the left and ran on through the deepening snow, their legs protesting at the increasing gradient beneath them. This time the cacophony seemed to remain on their right hand side, rather than continuing to circle them. After a few more seconds of rushing blindly through the snowfield, the sounds of the Wild Hunt began to fall away behind them as the group became lost to them in the noise of the storm. A few steps more, and the noise faded away completely. It was gone. They stopped, gasping for breath.

"Have they gone?" asked Evan through heavy laboured breaths. He realised that as they had given the hunt the slip, the wind seemed to have abated as well, and he no longer had to shout to be heard. The desperation in his voice was reflected on the faces of his companions.

"Unlikely," said Celyn, also gasping for breath. "It's the one night of the year when they are free to hunt, they will be out until the solstice has passed. Make no mistake, they'll be back, but at least for now we seem to have lost them."

"But what do they want?" asked Travis. The wind had dropped considerably now, and the driving snow had returned to a gentle but still heavy fall.

"What they want," said Celyn, "is me. You may yet live to regret your desire to help me."

"No we won't," said Liam, surprising himself with the renewed courage he felt now that the wind had dropped and the hunt was gone.

"Yes," added Evan, "we couldn't just leave you there - not in our own back garden!"

The absurdity of that statement was not lost on any of the brothers. They were after all, or at least as far as they knew, still in their own back garden. The realisation made him feel less afraid. The feeling was short-lived however, as a cold draught brushed the back of his neck ruffling his hair, and just at the very edge of audibility was the barest echo of pounding hooves. They all fell silent, straining to hear if the sound was real or imagined, and hoping against hope that if they stayed still, anything out there beyond the veil of snow would not notice them and move on. Another gust of icy air sent shivers down Evan's spine.

"I think the wind's picking up again," he said fearfully.

Another shot of adrenalin surged through him, as he realised that he was beginning to have to raise his voice again to be heard above the rising wind. Once more the distant sounds of shouting and barking reached them, and they were getting closer.

"We have to move," shouted Celyn, "Go!" The group were panicked again, and their collective "fight-or-flight" response spurred them into action, but just as they started to run once more into the snow, Liam called out: "Wait, over there, I thought I saw something."

"Well let's not hang around to find out what it is!" retorted Travis. "We need to get out of here." But even as he said it, the gale created a vortex in the snow storm, which allowed him to see a little further into the night, and for a brief moment, the weak glow of a distant firelight penetrated the wall of snowflakes before it was lost to sight again.

"Wait! I see it too," he screamed above the wind. "I think it's the house. This way, follow me!"
Travis battled forward against the wind, his arm raised over his face to try and protect it from the tiny daggers of ice that were being driven into it. The sounds of the hunt were much louder again now, and coming from directly behind them. The hunt was closing in again, and all they could do was run for the house. The group lunged forward as the rumbling of the horses' hooves and the frenzied baying of the pack got closer and closer. The howling was by now so loud in their ears that they must surely be run down at any minute. Absolute terror drove them blindly forward, as the sound of the hunt and the storm became almost too loud to bear. In another second, the hunt was upon them.

The group were caught. They threw themselves face down in the snow as the hooves of the charging horses bore down upon them. The riders whooped and hollered astride their steeds, working themselves up into a frenzy. Over their heads, hooves clattered and roared like a train and the teeth of a hundred hounds snapped and slavered at them as they curled into defensive balls in the snow waiting for the inevitable, horrific end that was surely moments away. Then, just as their time seemed to be up, the Wild Hunt continued straight over the top of them and on to be lost in the snow, leaving behind rapidly fading echoes of the awful sounds that just seconds before had spelt out their certain doom.

Liam was the first to react. "Wait," he said through a mouthful of snow, "did they just fly right over the top of us?"

Evan raised his head to see the final vortex of the hunt's passage spiral away into the distance, once again clearing the way for a quick glimpse of weak orange-red illumination in the distance.
"Who cares?" he shouted. "There's the house, run before they come back again."

Liam and Travis reached down to where Celyn lay in the snow, grabbed an arm each and hauled her to her feet, and then they were running again. In a few more seconds the light from the house windows was able to penetrate the wall of snow, and they ran on with renewed strength up the path beside the top retaining wall and skidded right on to the patio at the back of the house, dragging Celyn behind them. Evan reached the back door first and flung it open, waiting just outside until he was sure that everyone was accounted for before diving into the house and quickly slamming it shut behind him.

Finding themselves suddenly out of any immediate danger,

the four of them collapsed onto the floor of the living room, wheezing and gasping for breath.

9 INSIDE

Travis was the first to recover, and scrambled up off the floor, clearly still awash with adrenaline. "Are they gone? Celyn! Are they gone?" He asked urgently through rasping breaths. The exertion of their escape was still causing him to gasp for each breath and his heart pounded in his chest harder than he could ever remember. Liam and Evan were starting to get up off the ground as well now, and with heaving breaths they staggered to their feet. Evan stood up a little too quickly, and had to support himself on the mantelpiece while he waited for a sudden dizzy spell to pass.

Celyn was still sitting on the floor and hadn't answered, so Travis tried again, this time a little more forcefully: "Celyn!"

"What? Yes, yes!" She replied, her shoulders rising and falling as she took several deep breaths to replenish the oxygen that she used up in replying. "Yes, we'll be safe in here."

The calm inside the house and the warmth of the fire was in stark contrast to the freezing temperature and chaos that they had endured in the garden moments before. Now that he had a little time to adjust to his surroundings, Liam looked around and it occurred to him that all of the lights in the house were off, and the only illumination came from the fire, and the glow from a couple of battery-powered Christmas decorations. "Looks like we've had a power cut," he announced.

"A power cut!" said Travis. "You are joking aren't you? Surely that's the least of our worries. Weren't you with us outside just now? What the hell was that all about?"

"Alright Travis, calm down. It's just an observation, maybe there is some connection."

"This is getting crazier by the minute, we could have been killed out there, in our own back garden! What the hell is going on?"

When they were being pursued by the hunt Travis had been able to remain calm enough in the face of extreme stress to guide them all back to the house, but now that they were clear of any immediate danger the bizarreness of the situation was starting to affect him. Liam could see that someone else was going to have to take the lead for a while in order to give Travis a break.

"Ok, ok," said Liam, "Celyn said we be safe inside, and that does seem to be the case. I'm going to look out of the window. Just wait here."

"Whoa, hang on!" said Evan, eyes still wide with fear. "You're not going to the back door are you?"

"It's ok," said Liam with more calmness than he felt. "I'm sure they've gone, it sounds like the wind has died down again. And anyway, regardless of whether they are still out there or not, me checking isn't going to change anything is it?"

He cautiously made his way to the double doors in the bay off the main sitting room. With his heart racing, and terrified of what he might see, he carefully moved one of the curtains aside, just enough to allow him to peek through. Outside the snowfall continued, but other than that, everything appeared to be normal. There was no sign of the Wild Hunt or any other unusual activity, and the wind had dropped off to nothing again.

Satisfied that there was no imminent threat, Liam slipped through the curtains for a better look outside. "It looks quiet out there now," he called back to the others in the living room.

"We'll be safe enough now we are out of the storm," said Celyn. "We just need to wait it out in here until the solstice passes."

"Wait, what?" said Liam from behind the curtains. "So that's all we need to do? If we stay out of the storm, we are safe?"

Liam pulled his phone from his pocket to check the time to see just how much longer they would have to wait. He tapped irritatedly a few times at the illuminated screen before announcing to the others: "Whenever that might be! The clock app on my phone has crashed."

"We are safe out of the storm because they ride with the storm, so if there is no storm they are not nearby, but the main reason we are safe here is because they can't dismount," said Celyn. "Anywhere that they can't easily get to on horseback is safe from them."

Turning around, Liam walked back into the living room, and despite the fear that he was still feeling, was dumbstruck by the sight of Celyn standing in front of the fire. Nothing could have looked more incongruous than to have what appeared to be a living, breathing character from a fairy tale, standing in the middle of their typically untidy front room. For the first time in his life he became aware of the mess, and an acute sense of embarrassment filled him. "This," he thought, "must be why mum and dad keep moaning about cleaning up."

In the firelight, Celyn was even more beautiful than she had appeared outside in the snow. Her dark hair cascaded down on to her shoulders and spilled down over her back. To describe it as brown would be like describing polished gold as yellow. The colour was deep and rich and run through with highlights of red and gold, and it shone like satin. The oddly pointed tips of her ears poked through just below the band of silver that encircled her head.

As she turned to take in her new surroundings, firelight flashed from the perfectly fashioned silver leaves of a pendant hung from a chain around her neck. It was a simple sprig of holly, with blood red berries made of some Otherworldly gem that seemed to glow with an inner light.

Celyn's clothing, that had appeared so dark and heavy outside in the night, was revealed to be opulent, richly coloured velvet in the firelight. Intricate designs were traced upon her skirt and bodice in golden coloured thread. The deep red of her lips, Liam noted somewhere in his mind, contrasted most effectively with her clear pale skin. The effect was not lost on Evan and Travis either, who were both staring open mouthed at her. The effect of Celyn's presence on the brothers, combined with her innate ability to cloud the thoughts of those around her was enough to begin to take their minds off their fears for their safety.

Travis was caught off guard as Celyn turned towards him and caught him staring. That was when he noticed her eyes, which were the blue green of deep glacial ice. She flashed him a smile and Travis flushed red. Perhaps a little too quickly, he spluttered out a question to cover his embarrassment. "So why are they chasing you anyway?" he said. "What did the Wild Hunt want with you?"

"Well, the short answer is that the Wild Hunt serves a purpose. It's said that they only chase down wrongdoers and people who deserve it in some way, but that is clearly preposterous. Whenever someone was taken, people would look back over their life and find something they had done wrong, or something they regretted, and they'd say 'There you are! That's why they were taken!'. But it's just a way of justifying it, when the simple fact of the matter is that they love to hunt. But with the Wild Hunt in particular, I think there is more to it; they have been hunting for so long that they have become the spirit of the hunt, they simply can't do, or be anything else. But to really understand why they do what they do" said Celyn, "I'd better tell you the background of the Wild Hunt. Take a seat," she added; "this will take a little while, and as humans, you are going to have a hard time believing some of it. Although you do have one advantage over most other mortals in that you at least have now seen the hunt and lived to tell the tale."

"In that case, let me go and make a hot drink first," said

Evan.

"The kettle won't work," stated Travis. "The power's off, remember?"

"The cooker hob's gas, though," countered Evan, "and I'm absolutely freezing!" With a monumental act of will he tore himself away from the vision that was Celyn, and headed towards the kitchen. It was more than just leaving Celyn that made him reluctant to leave the living room. The lack of electric lighting and the memory of the hunt meant that even that simple journey felt laced with danger.

"Check the time while you are out there will you?" asked Liam, still trying to work out how much longer it would be until they could venture outside again.

Evan opened the door and entered the kitchen, the hairs on the back of his neck stood on end, and his eyes widened again all his senses strained to detect anything out of place. In a state of heightened alertness, he hurried to the cooker and pressed and turned one of the burner controls to provide some light. Nothing happened, instead of the expected clicking as the cooker tried to ignite the gas there was silence. A cold rush of fear flowed through him until he realised that because of the power cut there was no electricity to create a spark. Feeling a little foolish, and secretly glad that Celyn was not there to witness his jumpiness, he instead opened the cutlery drawer and retrieved a box of matches kept there for just this type of emergency.

A few moments later, Evan returned from the kitchen having filled the kettle, and left it to boil on the big range cooker.

"It'll be a few minutes," he stated taking a seat on the settee.

"Time?" queried Liam.

"Don't know," replied Evan. "The clock on the cooker is off as well."

"That," said Liam sarcastically, "would be because of the power cut! I meant for you to check the clock above the door. It runs on batteries."

"Alright, calm down," replied Evan, clearly a little annoyed and embarrassed at what he perceived to be Liam's attempt to make him out to be stupid in front of Celyn. "I'll check when the kettle boils." Then, turning to Celyn, he continued "The kettle will be ages, why don't you start telling us about the hunt?"

10 HERLA

"The story of the Wild Hunt is an old one," began Celyn, "even by the measurements of my people. Herla was king among humans, but it was so long ago now that I expect his name is all but unknown to you. No matter, in those days there was much more communication between your people and mine, and we were able to cross between worlds much more easily back then.

One day, King Herla had been out hunting in an unfamiliar part of the forest when he happened upon a very small man with a long bushy red beard riding on a goat. King Herla immediately recognised that the man was from the 'Otherworld', and knew to be careful around him, because beings from the Otherworld were known to be tricky. The little man told King Herla that he himself was also a powerful king amongst his own people, the dwarf race, and suggested that the two of them should make a deal. If King Herla invited him to his wedding, then in return the dwarf king would invite King Herla to his own wedding under the mountains when he married. After considering the offer for a while, King Herla could see no obvious harm in it, and agreed, and then the two parted ways. Shortly thereafter, the King fell in love. On his wedding day the dwarf king arrived, with many attendants, bearing fabulous gifts for King Herla and his bride. They brought so much food and drink that the King's own stocks were barely touched. The next day, the dwarves packed up and returned to their kingdom in the Otherworld. Another year passed, and King Herla and his wife had lived happily for all of that time. Then, one day, word arrived that the king of the dwarves was to wed, and King Herla prepared to travel to the Otherworld to fulfil his part of the agreement. Before he left, his advisors warned him to not to stay long, because time moves differently and unpredictably in the fairy realms."

After many days travelling, with his horses laden down with expensive gifts and the finest food and wines, the King's company arrived at a sheer cliff face. They passed through an opening in the cliff and began their long journey underground. Eventually they arrived in a huge cavern that was brightly lit by flaming torches."

King Herla and his company were treated very well indeed by the dwarves. There were long tables laden with more food than any man could hope to eat. Herla ate his fill, and was amazed by the rich flavours of the food; every different dish he tried contained new and exciting tastes that exploded across his tongue. You see flavour, in common with everything else, is much more intense in the Otherworld. Colours are brighter, sound is clearer and richer, and food has depths of flavour the like of which King Herla had never encountered before. Musicians played and King Herla listened awestruck as within each note that was played, he heard layer upon layer of ethereal harmonics. Now, as might be expected, King Herla became so absorbed with everything that was going on in the halls of

the dwarf king, that he stayed far longer than he should
have. In fact, by the time he left, he had stayed for three
whole days. Before he departed, the dwarf king gave Herla a
gift of a bloodhound and a warning that when he got home,
no man should dismount before the bloodhound jumped
down from the horse."

After travelling for a long time through the underground
tunnels of the dwarf Kingdom, King Herla and his
company approached the same opening in the cliff face that
they had passed through three days earlier. However, on
returning through they were amazed to find that the
landscape outside had transformed dramatically; where
there had been dense forest, there were now rolling fields.
King Herla stopped a man and asked him what had
happened to the kingdom. But the man could barely
understand a word that King Herla said. Eventually he
managed to communicate that the king was speaking in the
tongue of the ancient Britons, and that no one had spoken
that language for hundreds of years. Worriedly the king
asked after his wife. The man told him that he had heard of
a queen who had that name but that she had lived hundreds
of years ago, and had died of a broken heart when her
husband failed to return from a journey to the Otherworld.
You see, in the three days that had passed in the dwarf
Kingdom, three hundred years had passed on earth. On
seeing the effect that the news about the queen was having
on their king, a few of King Herla's company jumped down
from their horses to remonstrate with the man, but they
had failed to wait for the bloodhound to jump down first,
and they instantly crumbled away to dust."

From that day to this, King Herla's company are still
waiting for the bloodhound to jump down from the horse.
Unable to dismount, they ride as the Wild Hunt. Always
accompanied by bad weather, they tear through the storm-

Rob Beck

torn skies, waiting for the day they can finally catch up with the King of the Dwarves again. In your world, they are only active around the winter solstice, riding through the winter skies chasing down their quarry."

"So why are they chasing you?" asked Travis.

"As far as I can tell, they just live for the hunt. Until the day when they are able to dismount, there is really nothing else for them to do. Generally unbelievers and the unwary are particularly vulnerable because they are unlikely to hide away during storms and the hunt will snatch them up from the ground as they course overhead."

Just then an insistent whistling from the kitchen announced that the kettle had boiled. Evan went back into the kitchen and returned a few minutes later with a tray of mugs of steaming hot chocolate topped with a generous swirl of spray cream.

"What's got into you?" asked Travis on his return. "Making drinks for everyone, no bargaining, no conditions attached, and no moaning!"

"Oh, grow up will you!" replied Evan. "I can always tip yours away again if you like!" Despite the bizarre events that had just taken place in the garden, things seemed to be returning to normal pretty quickly once they were back in the familiar environment of the house.

"Don't be getting too comfortable," said Liam. "Things were seriously weird outside don't forget, and from what Celyn said, it doesn't sound like normal service is going to be resumed anytime soon. What is the time by the way Evan?"

78

"Still don't know," replied Evan. "That clock has stopped too; it still says six o'clock, which was about when we got back from shopping and that was hours ago."

"Just a moment," said Celyn, with a worried tone in her voice, "are you saying that none of your clocks are working?"

"Well, only the one in the kitchen," said Evan. "We don't know about the others because the power is out."

"But he said his clock 'something or other' stopped working while he was looking out of the window," Celyn said indicating Liam.

"That was the clock on his mobile phone," Travis informed her. "We can't check on the internet either because the power cut has knocked the router out."

"I think I know how King Herla felt when he returned to Earth," said Celyn. "It sounds like you are speaking a foreign language! Don't you have any other clocks in this house?"

"Only on the phones," said Evan, checking his own, "and mine has crashed too."

Thus far, Celyn had managed to infer that a 'phone' was the small block that the teenagers held onto constantly. Evan's can't have been badly damaged in the crash because it still retained its rectangular shape, and continued to glow happily when he stroked it. Putting aside her struggles with the many changes to the language of this world since she was last here, Celyn pressed them for more information.

"This is important," said Celyn. "Think carefully, do you believe that all of the clocks in this house have stopped?"

"Now you mention it, the old guy in the second hand shop said that his clock seemed to be running slowly when we were out in the town earlier. Do you think that's relevant?" said Liam.

Celyn was beginning to look very concerned now.

"I think it might well be," she replied, "and if it is, then we have bigger problems than simply being pursued by the Wild Hunt!"

11 PLAN

"Bigger problems than being hunted by a bunch of crazy dudes and their pack of mad dogs, on a Christmas day-out from fairyland?" said Travis incredulously, "I would seriously love to hear how we can have bigger problems than that!"

"Well, allow me to enlighten you then," said Celyn picking up on Travis's sarcastic tone. "King Herla and the Wild Hunt can only ride out until the solstice; once the solstice passes the hunt will not return for another year - understand that?"

"Yeah," replied Travis.

"All the clocks seemed to have stopped - understand that?"

"Err yes," said Travis, a little less confidently, now that the implications of what Celyn was saying were beginning to dawn on him.

"We talk about the winter solstice as if it was the whole day, but it is actually a definite point in time, the exact midpoint of winter. Now, I think that King Herla may have managed to find a way to stop time, and if he has, then we will never progress beyond the solstice. If that happens, the hunt will be able to continue forever, or until the bloodhound finally jumps down from his horse," said Celyn, and then added: "Understand that?" for good measure.

"Yes, ok, I think I get what you mean," replied Travis.

Then Celyn smiled at him again, and all the acrimony dissolved. Celyn had to remind herself that although these kinds of events were commonplace to her, they must seem very strange, and difficult to believe, to modern day humans.

Suddenly a thought occurred to Evan and he spoke up: "Wait a minute, we do have another clock! Remember, a couple of Christmases ago? Our uncle bought us all LCD watches. The batteries in those last for years. I bet they are still working. I'm sure mine is in the bedroom on the chest of drawers. Hang on a second and I'll check." Evan walked through into the dining room and up the darkened stairs into the bedroom. Even though there was no light in the house, the thick covering of snow outside reflected enough light through the open bedroom curtains to just illuminate the room. In the semi-darkness Evan retrieved the watch and pressed the small silver button on its side. The little display flicked on, silhouetting the liquid crystal digits. His initial relief that the watch was still working, and that time was therefore still passing by normally, was soon dashed as he took note of the time. The display read "18:00", exactly the same time as the clock in the kitchen. He returned downstairs with the news.

Celyn looked worried: "Then it's true. We are going to have to accept that somehow Herla has managed to stop time."

"So are you saying," said Evan, "that time is just going to freeze at the solstice, and that we are going to be stuck like this, in the middle of winter forever?"

"Well, unfortunately yes," Celyn replied. "Although if the hunt catches up with you, you won't have to endure it for long!"

"That's not funny," said Liam. "There must be something we can do."

"Well, they must have used some ancient and powerful magic to do something like this," mused Celyn. "There might be a way to undo it if we knew what they had done, but I unfortunately have no idea. I have never known anything like it. Do any of you have any suggestions?"

The thought of anyone using any kind of magic, ancient and powerful or otherwise was difficult enough for the brothers to accept. So the idea that they might be able to do something about it made no sense at all to them.

"Hardly," said Travis, "before tonight, the most unusual thing that had ever happened around here was when it didn't rain for three days straight last summer. So we've have had absolutely nothing to prepare us for the serious level of weirdness that has kicked in since this evening."

"Yeah, he's right," said Evan. "I don't see how we are going to be able to help at all."

"Wait a moment," said Liam, "Back it up a bit. You said

'ancient and powerful magic', right?"

"Yes," replied Celyn.

"Well, when we were in that junk shop in the town earlier, the owner was warning us about the solstice, and being careful about what we said."

"True," said Evan, "but we haven't said anything, nothing that could cause all this, and anyway, Celyn said it was all down to King Herla."

"Yes, I know," replied Liam, "but that isn't what I mean. He also had a lot of old books about mid-winter festivals, I mean really old books. I couldn't even make sense of the titles of some of them, but there was one that I can remember."

"Go on," said Celyn becoming more interested.

"It was called 'A Study of Ancient Solstice Magic'. I mean it's got to be worth at least looking at, right? You said we might be able to undo it if we knew what magic they used, well that could be the place to find out."

"It's a good idea," said Travis, "but in case you have forgotten, it's still snowing out there, and earlier on we couldn't even find our way around our own back garden. On top of that, King Herla and his merry men are still out there, intent on hunting Celyn down, and who knows what else. How on earth are we going to make it into town?"

"I could probably help with that," said Celyn. The brothers turned to look at her as she held up the silver and gemstone holly pendant she was wearing. "This was given to me by my father when I was a child," she said, and then added: "which by your reckoning, would have been many hundreds of years ago."

"So how is it going to help us out there?" asked Travis nodding his head towards the back door, in case anyone was in any doubt about where 'out there' was.

"Well," she said, "it has the ability to illuminate anything that has crossed between the realms. So if there is anything in this world that has come from elsewhere, we'll be able to see it. It's hard to explain exactly what it does if you haven't used one. You'll see what I mean when we get outside again. But I think that the snowfall may actually work in our favour, because the Hunt will be just as blinded by it as we are, but we'll have the advantage in that we'll see them coming."

"Well I suppose that's settled then," said Liam, "and it's not as though we have any better ideas."

12 SNOW-BLIND

A short time later, they had assembled in the hallway that at some point in the past had been a walled yard used to store coal, and now, with the addition of a sloped roof, served as a utility room. Evan unlocked the front door, pulled it open, and nervously peered out. The wind had died away and the world outside was silent once more. The snow was still falling, and was now so thick, that they could see no further than a few feet in front of them. Evan stepped cautiously out into the night, followed closely by Celyn and Liam.

When it was Travis's turn to venture outside, he found himself unable to move, as the memories of the terror they had experienced in the back garden poured over him in an irresistible flood, threatening to drown him. His mind kept replaying the image of the wild hunt that they had seen in the lightning flash. Despite his efforts to conquer the fear, the colour drained from his face and he was rooted to the spot. His breathing became rapid and shallow.

"Whoa, whoa, wait a minute!" he called to the others breathlessly, "There must be another way to do this. Don't you remember what happened in the garden? The second we step out there, they'll be able to get us again."

"We don't really have any choice, do we?" said Evan, "If we don't do this, we'll be stuck like this forever."

"Well, maybe we should go back inside, just for a few minutes, to think about it," said Travis. It sounded desperate and he knew it.

Evan understood why Travis felt the way he did, and replied: "Look, it's not stormy, so the hunt isn't nearby, and anyway, we aren't really safe in the house, it just feels like it. Think about what will happen if we wait it out in the house. We have no power, sooner or later we are going to run out of food. And what about mum and dad and all our mates? We'll probably never see any of them again."

Travis knew that Evan was right; he had known it all along. He didn't want to stand there scared and shaking in the doorway. What he wanted to do was be brave and get out there and try and do something about the situation that they had been forced into, but his body wouldn't comply. He was frozen by fear. Travis resolved to try again, and swallowing hard, he forced the images from his mind and braced both hands on the door frame. He tried to calm his rapid breathing with slow, deliberate exhalations, and instructed his feet to move, but his legs just shook beneath him, and his knees threatened to buckle.

"I don't think I can,' he said fighting against deep feelings of embarrassment, "I mean I'm trying, but just can't do it."

Even turned and started to take a step back to help him, but

Celyn placed a gentle but firm had on his arm: "Give him a chance, he'll handle all this better if he can overcome this on his own."

"Come on Trav," said Evan. "We can't do this without you. We wouldn't have escaped from them when we were in the garden, if it hadn't been for you. You were the only one who was able to remain calm enough to think about what was happening. We need you."

Celyn could see that Travis was struggling with the fear of failure as well as the fear of the hunt. She also suspected that appearing frightened in front of her might be having an effect too. "Travis," she said, "I know it's frightening, but think about it this way: if you can get through this, you won't have failed at all, you'll have triumphed. Most people think that those that can take these things in their stride are brave, but they're wrong, it's not bravery if you aren't scared. Brave people are scared, really scared like you are now, but they do it anyway. You can do this!"

What Celyn said made a lot of sense to Travis, especially the idea that true bravery was only possible in the presence of fear. He made another attempt to walk through the doorway, and although it felt like it was happening to someone else, he finally managed to force one shaking leg into motion, and stepped outside.

Once he had made the transition from the safety of the house into the snow, he found that although he was still frightened, something about the act of defying his fear made it seem a little easier to continue, but not much.

"Ok," said Travis, "so what now? We can't see a thing in front of us."

Liam answered: "As long as we keep walking in a straight line from the front door we are bound to hit the park wall on the other side of the road; it's no more than about fifteen feet away, and don't forget we also have Celyn's necklace."

They set off into the snow. After a few paces, they were back to feeling as if they were trapped in a snow globe once again. Evan looked back to the house and was shocked to find that already he could see no sign of it, he suddenly felt very exposed. In front of them, the veil of snowflakes stayed resolutely a few feet ahead as they moved, retreating further into the night with each step they advanced, whilst at the same time closing in treacherously behind them. Celyn lifted the holly pendant and held it out in front of her, the chain still around her neck. But as far as any of the brothers could tell, at that moment it seemed to be achieving very little. They walked forward a few paces more. The only sound in the silent world was the soft creaking of the newly fallen snow compressing beneath their feet with every step. Then to everyone's relief the wall around the park came into view.

"There it is!" said Evan, surprising himself with the relief he felt from encountering something as mundane as a concrete wall.

"You can't count on everything being where you expect it to be," cautioned Celyn. "We were lucky this time, but there was a reason why it was so easy for you to get lost in the garden, and it wasn't just because of the snow. At the solstice, your world and mine are much closer than at any other time, which I think is why the hunt were able to chase me through. We are drifting between our two worlds, and as we do they overlay and merge with each other. Sometimes we are more present in my world, and at others we are more present in yours. The snow just makes it hard to tell which one we are more in."

"Oh, that's great!" Said Travis, "like we don't have enough problems already!"

"Hang on though," said Liam, "that didn't happen in the house, everything was exactly the same. Well, apart from the clocks."

"That's because it's easier to fix your place in one world when you are surrounded by familiar things," replied Celyn. "I don't want to worry you anymore, but we are likely to drift deeper into my world as we approach the solstice. You should probably prepare yourselves for the likelihood that things are going to become considerably stranger."

"Well," said Liam with a note of determination in his voice, "things are going to get pretty strange anyway if King Herla successfully manages to stop the solstice from happening. Let's get going and see if we can do something about it."

The company turned to the right, and moved on, keeping the wall on their left, and being careful to stay within touching distance of it. After a short time the wall made a ninety degree turn to the left as it continued around the boundary of the park, and they followed. Other than the constant worry that the Hunt might rematerialise at any moment, this first part of the journey was reasonably straightforward and uneventful as they began to make progress up the lane. When the wall turned left once again to continue across the eastern edge of the park, the group stopped.

"Ok," said Liam, "we're going to have to cross to the other side of the road if we are going to stay close to a wall. The wall around the old school is over there, and it will lead us up to Varley Lane."

"There are houses on this side of the road though," protested Evan. "Why don't we just follow them?"

As Evan had said, the lane was in fact, bordered on both sides: on the side they were currently on by a row of houses, and on the other by a high stone wall around the school.

"I just think we'd be safer by the wall." reasoned Liam. "We don't want to accidentally wander into someone's garden or driveway, we'd soon be lost."

Liam's logic made sense, so leaving the park behind, they ventured out once again into the snow in an attempt to reach the opposite wall. After a few more anxious paces, it loomed out of the snow at them. The next obstacle they would face would be crossing Varley Lane, the small road that separated them from the cattle market car park - then their real challenge would begin. The car park was a large expanse of tarmac, at least two hundred yards across, with very few features in it at all, which they would have to cross if they were to make it into town. Secretly, each of the brothers was dreading crossing the car park. As ridiculous as that sounded, it was a much bigger undertaking than simply navigating around the garden.

They reached the top of the lane, and the high stone wall that they were following curved gently away to their right. This indicated to the group that it was time for them to cross the road and commence the journey across the car park.

"Ok, this is where we need to cross the road," said Evan,

mostly to Celyn, as the others currently had a pretty good idea of where they were. Although none of them were under any illusion that that could not all change as soon as they crossed the road in front of them. They set out across the road, but had taken only a pace or two when a distant howling reached their ears. The group stopped, terrified that it could be the Wild Hunt returning, for it was clearly the sound of a creature not of their world, but something about the quality of the sound was different. And when a few seconds later it sounded again, it was even further away. The group continued into the snow, and as they expected, within a few footsteps their world was once again reduced to a little sphere a handful of feet across. Cautiously, they made their way across the road, being very careful not to deviate from the straight line that should take them to the ramp up to the cattle market, or if they angled off, should at least cause them to intersect with the earth bank that ran to either side of the ramp. As they crossed the road, Liam noticed something odd about the falling snow, and voiced his concerns to the others.

"Guys!" he said, "I don't think the snow is falling as fast."

"Well that's a good thing isn't it?" said Travis. "It's always stormy when the hunt is around."

"True," said Liam. "But that's not what I meant. There is still just as much of it, but it's actually falling slower - look."

"I don't know," said Evan, "it looks pretty much the same to me."

"You have to look up a bit and try and pick out a single snowflake," said Liam, "then follow it down, you'll see what I mean. It seems to take too long to fall to the ground."

"He's right," said Travis after trying Liam's technique. "And is it just me, or can you kind of see the flakes better? I mean, I get that snowflakes are six sided crystals, but I've never been able to actually 'see' that with my own eyes before."

Upon examination, it became clear to the rest of the group what he meant: each individual flake was a thing of beauty. They were exactly as they were supposed to be, but more so: more real, more detailed, and more crystalline, and they hung and sparkled and slowly turned in the air. The group had all been concentrating so hard on maintaining a straight course, and the change in the rate of the snowfall had been so gradual, that none of them had noticed.

"We have shifted further into the Otherworld," said Celyn. "Everything there is more intense. Beauty is amplified, but unfortunately so are the less beautiful aspects of my world. And as for snow falling more slowly, well that's not so good," she continued. "I think it's another sign that time is slowing down, and the nearer we get to the solstice, the slower it's going to get. Come on we need to be moving faster."

As if in response to Celyn's comments about the ugly side of the Otherworld, another distant howl echoed mournfully across the snow-blanketed car park.

13 DARKNESS

"They have found Celyn," said a voice in the dark. His words echoed back at him giving shape to a vast unseen cavern.

"Oh dear, that's most unfortunate," came a disembodied reply.

"It's worse than that I'm afraid, they have left the house and headed out into the snow."

"'Tis of no consequence, the Hunt will catch up with them soon enough if they are out in the snow."

"The Hunt!" spat the first. "It was the Hunt that drove Celyn to them in the first place. I'd be happier leaving them to get lost in the snow than to trust them to that parade of freaks."

"What do you think they are planning?"

"That is my concern; I don't know," replied the first. "If the humans were on their own then I would think nothing of it, but now She is with them the game has changed rather. I can only assume that they have a very good reason to venture out. The humans have encountered the Hunt now after all."

"Yes, yes, I see what you mean. You don't think they are searching for it, do you?"

"Well, if they are then they are headed in the wrong direction. But no, they don't know anything about it. With luck they will become lost in the snow, and that will be an end to this little inconvenience, but to be sure I am going to need you to follow them and see what they are up to. That shouldn't prove too much of a problem to you with your special talents should it?"

"Oh no," said the second happily.

A little glowing flicker of glee wavered over his skin as he considered the prospect of a little revenge against the humans. In the darkness of the place they were in the peculiar moving pattern of bio-luminescence resembled the light of a candle chasing jagged shadows across a hewn rock face.

"Well, just keep on eye on them, and don't get too close. Hopefully you won't have to do anything at all. Meet me back here when you know something."

14 HUNTED

The group made their way out across the open car park. Within a few tens of feet the terrain became much less easy to traverse. Out in the open, beyond the sheltering effect of the old school buildings, the driving winds that had accompanied the Wild Hunt had sculpted the snowfield into a strange and alien landscape. Their progress was drastically slowed by monstrous snow-dunes that arced up before them like sea-creatures from a dream, breaking the surface of an unexplored ocean. As each new dune loomed out of the wall of whiteness before them, they had to concentrate hard to retain a sense of in which direction they were heading as they skirted around its edge, only to be immediately presented with another to clamber around.

By the time they had navigated to the midpoint of the car park so much time had passed that the snow's rate of fall was barely perceptible. Moving through the dense, but almost static snow was a curious experience. To Evan it was reminiscent of a computer generated 3D scene: every flake was frozen in place in the air, but as they moved and their viewpoint changed, the crystals appeared to wheel and twist around each other into new positions until the next time the group paused. With each new step forward the flakes closest to them were swirled around by the eddies and vortices of their passage, but resolutely refused to fall any closer to the ground.

Celyn had been leading them for some time, holding the pendant from her necklace up ahead of her. The brothers were still not sure of exactly how this was helping when suddenly in the distance the merest impression of a shadow stirred. Strangely, the movement gave the impression of being quite a bit further away than they felt they could see, which was limited by the dense wall of almost stationary snowflakes. As he strained to make out the source of the movement, Evan felt the hairs on the back of his neck stand up, and a shot of adrenaline surged through him. He glanced nervously towards Travis and could see by his brother's fear-widened eyes that he too was feeling the same way. Celyn stopped dead, and motioned for Liam, Evan and Travis not to make a sound. In the light of Celyn's necklace, a shadowy creature up ahead stopped and raised its head, scenting the air. After a few seconds, apparently satisfied that there was nothing of interest around, it turned and began to move away from them, fading away into the snow as it moved just beyond the reach of the holly pendant. Celyn turned and whispered to the brothers: "That was close. I'd say that Herla must have loosed some of the hounds to cover more ground in trying to locate us. At least it means he doesn't have a very clear idea of where we are. Fortunately, because of this," Celyn said, indicating the pendant on the end of her necklace, "he still doesn't. We could see further through the snow than it could."

"Well, why didn't it work anywhere else when we were lost?" asked Evan, rather more loudly than he had intended, and instantly regretting it.

Celyn looked around anxiously, certain that the sound of Evan's voice would alert Herla's hound to their location, but after a few seconds had passed and nothing had happened, she relaxed a little.

"Sorry," mouthed Evan. "I forgot."

"We must be deeply immersed in the Otherworld now." Celyn replied. "The pendant illuminates things from one world that are present in the other, so the more we merge with my world the stronger the effect will be as we encounter more things that have crossed the boundary."

Suddenly they became aware of a distant snarling sound. Apparently they had not been as lucky as they thought. The noise did not stay far off for long though, and it quickly increased in volume.

"It's on to us!" hissed Celyn, and holding one finger in front of her lips to indicate that they should be silent, she gestured frantically with her other hand for them to move to the right. Over the course of this bizarre evening, the brothers had learned to trust Celyn's judgement, and immediately they started to move. Now aware that the creature had heard them, the crumpling of each step as it compressed the deep snow beneath them sounded unnaturally loud, surely loud enough to guide the animal straight to them. At one point as they moved, Evan looked downward and was surprised to notice through his terror that they were crossing a set of small footprints similar to those he had seen in the garden. He resolved to consider the possible implications of this development at a later time, at the moment they had more pressing concerns. The snarling of the hunting hound as it closed them down was increasing in volume when Celyn suddenly stopped.

Turning to the three brothers she mouthed for them to remain still and quiet. Seconds later the creature entered the scope of the pendant, first as a faint shadow, but soon in horrifying detail as it bounded seemingly effortlessly across the summit of a dune before skidding to a halt at precisely the place they had been standing just a few moments before. It snapped at the air around it with vicious looking jaws for a few frantic moments before stopping to look around once more. The group felt terrifyingly exposed being so close to the hound, able to see and hear it, but unable to be seen. After several seconds of trying to suppress his breathing, Liam sucked in a lungful of cold air as slowly as quietly as he could, but even that sounded loud to him. Although he exhaled in as controlled a manner as possible, his breath swirled the snowflakes closest to his mouth around, and he felt sure that the beast would see them.

The hound froze, and then purposefully turned its head until it was facing directly at Liam. Gradually it started to pace towards him. Liam's heartbeat thumped in his ears and his breath quavered in his throat as he tried to stay calm, but still the animal advanced. With one more pace, it broke through the barrier of snowflakes that been their only protection. Staring at Liam, the hound lowered its head slightly, flattened its ears against its head and snarled menacingly. Involuntarily, Liam took a few slow steps backwards. The animal matched him pace for pace.

"Liam, stop!" hissed Celyn.

He took his eyes of the hound for a second and risked a glance over to her and realised his mistake; by stepping backwards, he had allowed the animal to get between him and the rest of the group. Sensing its success, the hound took no notice of Celyn, and continued to advance on

Liam. He had no choice now but to retreat. After another few steps, he found himself backed into the concave face of a snow-dune and was unable to move any further. The hound prepared to take another step closing the gap between it and its prey, when a strange noise caused it to stop. The animal froze in position, but did not take its eyes from Liam. In the distance another shape appeared in the glow of Celyn's holly necklace; a rider on horseback. The way that the hunting hound reacted to the sound made by the rider left the group in no doubt that the new arrival was not there to help them. Slowly and deliberately the rider closed in on them until it too was visible without the aid of the holly necklace.

Long ago the rider may have been a woman, but hundreds of years of riding with the hunt had taken its toll. Her skin was windburned and leathered, and drawn tight across the bones of her skull. Her long hair was matted and in places burned down to her scalp. Her clothes, in common with the other members of the hunt that they had glimpsed earlier, were tattered and scorched. The effect was terrifying, and the group stood open mouthed in shock. Liam's eyes widened in fear as he searched frantically but vainly with his hands over the snow dune for the smallest chance of escape. The rider turned her fearsome gaze on Liam, and guided the horse in closer.

She opened her mouth and emitted an odd keening whine that started so highly pitched that it was almost beyond hearing, and rapidly descended through almost the whole audible spectrum. The dog's ears pricked up alert for instructions. She appeared about to continue, when she abruptly stopped. A look of confusion briefly passed across her face, and she sat upright in the saddle. Turning her head, she scanned around for a few moments as if looking for something, then returned her attention to Liam.

An all consuming fear began to flow through Travis again, threatening to turn his limbs to jelly, but Celyn's counsel came back to him, and he resolved that this time he would not be struck immobile. This time he would act. Travis had about enough of threats against his family. He had had enough of these creatures invading his world and terrorising people. And he had had enough of being made to feel bad about himself. As he thought about these things, his fear began to transform into a raging anger, and the same hormone that had caused his limbs to shake uselessly earlier now charged them with super-human energy. Just as he had done when they were being pursued by the hunt, Travis entered the same state of mind that he had experienced in the garden earlier, if the concept of earlier really made sense anymore. The outcome did not look promising, but the way Travis saw it was that if he did nothing then, at the very least, Liam was going to be captured, or worse, and the same fate probably awaited them all. He could either let that happen, or he could try and do something about it. He might not succeed, but how was that any worse than the position they were in now? Resolved to act, Travis found himself in a calm and calculating place and he assessed the situation. Free now of mind numbing fear, he noticed that, the rider appeared to be intermittently distracted by something. He also noticed that the dog's attitude had changed when the rider arrived; it was now totally under her control. He doubted it would do anything without her authority. He was sure that if she became distracted again, he could move towards her without her seeing and without the dog attacking him.

The rider appeared to take stock of the situation; although the hound had cornered one of her quarry, the others were in a position from where they could possibly escape. Again she made a sound, and this time Travis could discern recognisable words within the strange frequency changes. She was instructing the hound to stay. The dog hunkered down lower and a slow growl rattled threateningly from deep within its throat at Liam. She turned her head to look in the direction of Celyn, Evan and Travis, but as she did so, her eyes became distant and she appeared to lose concentration again. Apparently confused, the rider turned slowly in her saddle and surveyed the area around her.

Travis seized his chance, when the rider had turned as far from them as she could, and without giving Celyn or Evan an opportunity to stop him, he sprinted free of the rest of the group. As he ran, he stooped and grabbed a handful of snow; the only weapon to hand, and hurled it at the rider.

"Leave my brother alone you bitch!" he shouted as the snowball exploded against the back of her head.

In an instant she reacted. With a level of control honed over hundreds of years, horse and rider turned to face Travis and reared up in preparation to gallop towards him in one flowing movement. As they turned, she issued a wailing command to the hound, and with a parting snarl at Liam it turned and raced after the horse.

Travis of course was expecting and hoping for a reaction such as this, and was already disappearing ahead of them into the snow.

"Trav, no!" Liam called out in panic, but it was too late, Travis had gone.

At the sound of Liam's voice the rider pulled up sharply on her horse's reins causing it to skid to a halt as its rear legs temporarily gave way beneath it, showering snow ahead of them. Then, having apparently thought better of giving up the chase, she started to urge the horse forward again. The animal had just regained its footing when once more she started to look around herself in confusion, as if she had no idea where she was. In the sudden silence they could just hear Travis's footsteps fading to the distance. The sound was enough to break the rider's confusion, and she resumed the chase again, disappearing into the night after Travis.

15 GONE

For a few moments, Liam, Evan and Celyn remained silent and motionless, dumbstruck by the events of the previous few minutes.

Liam was the first to react: "What the hell?" he began, as a tight knot formed in his stomach. Without pausing for thought he launched into a run and sprinted into the snow after Travis.

"Liam! Stop!" commanded Celyn. "We can't risk you being lost too, and you will be as soon as you are out of sight."

Liam skidded to a halt just before he disappeared from view.

"Ok, but in that case we all go," he replied urgently, looking over his shoulder as he half turned to face Celyn and Evan. And hurry up! The longer we wait the less chance we'll have of catching them!"

Celyn and Evan jogged the few feet to where Liam waited and together they raced into the darkness following the confused trail left by Travis and his pursuers.

They ran almost blindly, their attention focused on the small arc of ground immediately ahead of them that was all they could see before the ground and air blended together into a featureless whiteout. Their senses strained for any clue as to what might lie ahead, heightened in anticipation of the stunning pain they would feel if they were to collide with any obstacle that might come swinging out of the void towards them. In this enhanced state of awareness, brought on by the constant risk of injury, time became difficult for them to gauge, measured out in gasping breaths and muted thudding footfalls. Feeling as though he existed both in the moment, and outside of it at the same time, Evan fought against a rising feeling of frustration and helplessness; the blinding shroud of white that hemmed them in on all sides left him feeling powerless. For all he knew Travis could be almost within touching distance. If Evan could only see where he was he would pull that woman from her horse and show her what happened when you mess with someone's brother. True, he and Travis might fight and bicker, but that was family, it was expected, everyone knew that, but if someone else got involved, that was different, and if he could just see through this bloody snow, he would happily show her just how different!

The tracks that faded into view ahead of them in their little sphere of visibility veered wildly from one direction to another as Travis swerved to try and lose the rider. Although they couldn't see any distance at all, occasional muffled hoofbeats and agitated barking gave them an indication of where their quarry was. Often, this was not in the same direction that the tracks indicated.

"This way," called Evan to Liam and Celyn, as the sounds of the chase drifted into audibility again, leading them away from the trail in the snow, but towards the sounds of pursuit ahead of them. A few seconds later the noise abated again, and a wave of dread swept over Evan as he found himself leading the group through undisturbed snow towards apparently nothing. Then moments later, the smooth, featureless snow ahead was once again broken and churned by recent passage. No sooner had they recovered Travis's trail than a very large steep sided snow-dune lurched at them out of the whiteout and they had to quickly change course to avoid running straight into it. A large depression in the face of the dune suggested that Travis hadn't quite spotted it in time. However, they soon noticed that the trail continued around the right-hand side of the dune, and Liam, Evan and Celyn ran on.

The scream, when it came, sounded much further away than they would have expected, but there was no mistaking the voice. Colder than the chill air around them, an icy wave of shock surged along Liam and Evan's spines and even the burning rush of adrenaline flowing through their veins could not temper it. The pained cry continued for a second or two and then abruptly stopped. Evan's blood ran cold at the sound, and he fought to subdue a rising feeling of sickness. In panic and desperation Evan and Liam raced off again in the direction of the sound and began to pull away from Celyn, whose heavy clothing was not designed for strenuous exertion. The two brothers had accelerated to a pace that caused every breath to rasp painfully through their throats, and then the trail simply disappeared.

Liam slid to a halt and scanned desperately around in confusion: "What?" he said struggling to process this new information. "How can the tracks just stop?" But even as the words were leaving his mouth he knew: the horse had taken to the skies, and the absence of any more of Travis's footprints meant that he had gone with them.

Travis had been caught.

Evan's head span, and he was consumed by a feeling of overwhelming hopelessness. The sickness and shock that he felt at the events of the last few minutes threatened to overwhelm him. There was simply nothing they could do, Travis had been taken up into the air, and they could not follow. Minutes ago they had all been together, and now Travis was gone. In the strange blending of worlds that they found themselves in, who knew what that meant. Liam was struggling with the same worries. Useless guilt stabbed an accusing finger at him, reminding him that Travis had made his sacrifice to save him. Thoughts about how hard that must have been for Travis, given how reluctant he had been to risk encountering the hunt again when they left the safety of the house, kept surfacing in his mind, clamouring for attention.

"If only I hadn't been so stupid as to allow myself to become cornered!" he berated himself aloud. "This is all my fault."

"Then we would all have been caught," said Celyn flatly, recognising that Lam and Evan were in danger of falling apart, and hoping that speaking the plain truth would jolt them out of their spiralling depression. "We can't change what has happened. It's not your fault. It's not anyone's fault. If you want to blame anyone, I suggest that you blame the damned Hunt!"

"But what if he ends up like one of them?" Liam mused aloud, panic clearly audible in his words. "You saw that woman, she must have been human once!"

"Look, I know this is hard," counselled Celyn gently, "but we have to keep moving, we can't stay here. Your world is still in peril, we need to try and restore time."

"What's the point now Travis has gone?" Replied Evan despondently, shock clearly visible in his face as the colour drained from him. Even saying the words felt wrong. A hollow fear stole through every part of his being turning out the lights and whispering the awful truth that Travis was gone for good, and nothing would ever be the same. Suddenly, and quite outside of his control, Evan's legs buckled beneath him and he sat down heavily in the snow.

"Come on," continued Celyn, holding her hand out to Evan, "there will be time enough for grief. But for now, we have to do all we can to try and restore time. What Travis just did to protect Liam, gave us a chance, it could be our only one. We owe it to him to fight."

Evan reached up and took Celyn's hand. Even in his current state, her soothing influence flowed into him at her touch. With Celyn's assistance, he pulled himself to his feet. It was only then he realised that in chasing after Travis, they had lost any sense of where they were, and we're now utterly lost.

16 NAVIGATION

In the space of few short minutes the world had been thrown into turmoil. Travis had been taken and now, Evan realised, they were completely lost. He looked around, in all directions the snow hung motionless in the air as insubstantial as smoke, whilst at the same time obscuring everything more than a few feet away from view. A sudden feeling of claustrophobia and hopelessness consumed him, and he lashed out with his fists at the taunting snowflakes, wildly swinging his arms and roaring incoherently in frustration. Barely affected by his rage, the snowflakes were merely buffeted aside by the slipstream of his movements, and spiralled gracefully back into the space vacated by his flailing arms, cold and uncaring and beautiful.

"Damn this bloody snow!" He shouted, no longer caring whether or not anything would be drawn to them by the sound. A few moments later his shoulders began to spasm rhythmically, as he fought to stay in control.

Wordlessly, Celyn turned to him, wrapped her arms around

him and pulled him in close. Embarrassed and angry, Evan tried to pull away from her, but she felt warm and safe in a world that had stopped making any sense. Without saying anything to Evan or Liam, Celyn relinquished some of the control she had been maintaining over her ability cloud the thoughts of those around her. It wasn't something she did lightly, but to expect Evan and Liam to function in the face of all they had endured this evening would be without compassion. Evan felt himself relax in Celyn's embrace, and the horrors of this new world seemed to recede a little. Unseen, her influence flowed outward until Liam too was enveloped. Satisfied that she had relieved some of Evan's anxiety, Celyn released him and allowed her arms to fall slowly back to her sides. Evan was surprised at how much he didn't want that to happen considering how he had tried to pull away from her a few moments earlier.

"Wait,' he said, partially to stop her moving away from him and partially because he was starting to realise what she had done. "Did you just do that thing? You know the confusion thing that you said you could control."

"A little," she replied. "But only enough to help you cope, and just for a while."

Evan wanted to protest, but the thought of being thrown back into the despair of a few seconds earlier stopped him. He trusted Celyn's judgment enough to let it go. Now that the rawness of recent events had been eased a little, he voiced the concern that had recently occurred to him: "You do realise that we have no idea where we are, and no clue in which direction to go?"

Despite the calming effect of Celyn's aura, a renewed sense of dread descended on Liam as he began to appreciate what Evan was saying. They had entered the car park with a clear direction in mind, but being cornered by the hound and chasing after Travis meant that they were now totally lost. Liam scanned around him, but in every direction he looked, he could see nothing through the wall of snow. "What are we supposed to do now?" he asked, and then after a pause continued: "Celyn, what about your necklace, I don't suppose that could help could it?"

"Well, it can't hurt," she replied. Celyn took hold of the holly pendant and held it up in front of her. Nothing happened, every way she turned she could see nothing but white.

"I suppose all we can do is pick a direction and walk in as straight a line as we can," said Liam. I don't see how we have any other option, other than just staying here."

"I'd rather be moving anyway," said Evan. "Staying put won't achieve anything, except possibly getting us caught. At least if we're moving we might come across something that'll give us some idea where we are, like a ticket machine or a streetlight something."

"Alright," said Liam, "let's try this way then," and he led the remainder of the group out into the night once more.

As they trudged along, the snow, freed from the constraints of time and gravity, wafted and swirled around them. Occasionally, flakes would attach themselves to the front of their clothing rather than settling in the more usual location on the tops of their shoulders and heads, and gradually an even layer built up. Liam brushed away the thick coating that had covered the front of his jacket and trousers, as he had had to do numerous times since they set out. This time though, even this small act felt like a betrayal; attending to his own comfort when Travis was gone. In his misery Liam could only envisage two possible outcomes to the situation that Travis found himself in: At best his brother was enduring who knew what treatment at the hands of that company of horrors, with almost no hope of rescue. However, the worst, and if Liam was honest with himself the most likely, scenario was that Travis was in a place where nothing could help him anymore. The scream they had heard was so far away from where they would have expected it to come from that Travis must have shouted out after he had been caught. Recoiling at the thought, Liam turned to Celyn, and asked: "What do you think will happen to Trav? Will he become like them? What do they do to the people they catch?" The influence of Celyn's aura made it a little easier to talk about these things, and speaking of Travis as if he was still alive and had a future, however bleak, somehow made it seem more of a possibility, but saying the words aloud still amplified the hollow ache of loss.

"I'm sorry," she replied, "but I really don't know. It's difficult for me to say this to you, but as far as I know, no one who has been caught by the Wild Hunt has ever returned."

Evan felt his stomach knot despite Celyn's calming influence, but then, ahead of them, appearing out of the snow, he saw something that caused his mood to suddenly lift: "Look!" he said, pointing forwards. "Tracks!"

"What?" said Liam running forward. "He got away? But how? We saw where he was carried up into the air."

In his next few steps the truth was revealed to them. There were three distinct sets of foot-prints. These tracks were not left by Travis. In the short time they had been walking and talking and skirting around snow-dunes they had managed to circle completely around and we're now back where they had started.

This latest cruel trick of the snow was too much for Liam to cope with. The strange and alien world that they had been unwittingly dragged into suddenly seemed a much darker, colder and more frightening place. An ancient terror of the unknown welled up from deep within him. Like a shipwrecked sailor, cast into the black waters of an uncaring sea, each new realisation washed over him before he was able to draw breath after the previous one, filling his lungs with the bitter tang of hopelessness. Then, when he felt that he couldn't cope with it anymore an unexpected thought bobbed to the surface, it was not much, but it was something, and Liam mentally grabbed hold of it: "Wait a minute" he said, "What about Sat Nav?"

"Yeah, that's an idea," agreed Evan, "the Sat Nav on our phones - I can't believe we didn't think of it earlier."

Liam hurriedly pulled his smart phone from his pocket, pressed the 'Home' button to switch it on, and swiped left a couple of times until he located the icon for the 'Maps' app. With numb, fingers he tapped at the glowing pictogram. On command, the app expanded outward until it filled the whole screen. The glow from the phone lit up his face, revealing his disappointment in cold blue light. The little blue 'You are here' dot pulsated in the middle of a blank screen.

"Don't tell me," he said dejectedly to Celyn, "you don't have GPS satellites in Fairyland, do you?"

"We don't have 'what' in Fairyland?" said Celyn clearly confused, and by the tone of her voice, also a little irritated at Liam's use of the term 'Fairyland'.

"Never mind," said Liam, more kindly, realising that it was not Celyn's fault that the GPS system on his phone wasn't working. "Look, I'm sorry ok? I didn't mean to be rude," he added. "I can get a bit sarcastic when I'm feeling stressed, but it just doesn't work. It was a good idea, but it's not going to work, not here anyway."

"Wait a minute," said Evan. "We don't need satellite navigation do we?"

"Don't we?" replied Liam. "We're making a pretty bad job of navigating without it. We just walked round in a circle, in case you've forgotten."

"But we already know roughly where we are and where we are going. All we need to know is which direction to head in."

"So," said Liam. "How does that help us?"

"Well, we know our house is west of the car park, right? So all we need to know in order to get to the other side of it is which way is east."

"Compass!" said Liam suddenly understanding where Evan was going, before experiencing yet another deep pang of guilt at feeling excitement so soon after losing his brother. "The compass app. I bet they still have a magnetic North in Fairyland." And then added "Sorry Celyn, I mean 'The Otherworld'"

Evan switched to the compass app, and watched as the digital dial swung to point North. Then he gradually turned around until he was pointing due East.

"This way," he said, and they set off once more. With the aid of the compass, their progress was a lot quicker. They no longer had to worry about going off course when diverting around dunes of snow, or any other obstacles they encountered.

Within about another fifteen minutes of walking, the remainder of the company encountered a narrow pathway that descended an icy slope between two high walls.

"This is the alleyway that runs down beside that photography studio," Said Evan. "We are at the eastern end of the car park. It's not far to town from here."

They were just about to make their way into the alley, when the hazy shape of a figure moving rapidly up the slope towards them was revealed in the glow of Celyn's necklace. Fear surged through the brothers. Liam quickly realised that at the speed the figure was moving, it would only be a matter of seconds before it burst into view and they would be discovered. He grabbed Celyn's arm and tried to pull her to the right, in front of the photography studio, and away from the entrance to the alley. Celyn however seemed unconcerned, and placed her free hand over Liam's to stop him.

"It's alright," she said reassuringly. "I don't think this is someone we need to fear."

Although they could not make out any real detail yet, because they were still only able to see the approaching figure through the magic of the holly necklace, they could tell that it was human in form, although only about half the height of an average man. Quickly, the figure drew close enough for them to see without magical aid. Out of breath from his rapid waddle up the snowy slope, the man stopped and turned around.

"Come on, I've found them!" he called back down the slope between wheezing breaths.

Even felt another little jolt of fear. Despite Celyn's reassurances, this sounded ominous. Then without any warning glow from the necklace another, larger figure emerged from the snow.

17 THE LORD OF MISRULE

Of the two new arrivals that now stood at the entrance to the alleyway, the shorter was dressed in a manner so bizarre that Liam and Evan's initial fear of him evaporated instantly. On his head he wore a dog-eared purple paper crown of the type found in Christmas crackers. His clothing was brightly coloured, but old, and worn through in various places. The holes were patched over with materials that seemed to have been specially selected for their lack of coordination with the area they were intended to repair. About his waist was strung a battered wooden sword that even when it was new would surely have been of little use as a weapon.

The person standing next to him was Travis.

Liam and Evan could not contain themselves, and, overcome with relief and joy, ran at Travis. The resultant collision knocked him off his feet, and the three of them ended up on the ground rolling in the snow laughing. Liam grabbed a handful of snow and rubbed it playfully in

Travis's hair.

"You were freaking awesome!" He enthused. "The way you rushed that huntress and hit her with that snowball, it was like something from Black Ops!"

While the brothers were enjoying their reunion, Celyn turned to the oddly dressed little man, dropped into a deep respectful curtsey and said: "Well met, Your Majesty."

"Well met indeed, Lady Celyn!" replied the man. A broad smile spread across his face and he glanced shyly downward and scraped the toe of one battered boot backwards and forwards through the snow in a manner such as a child might, as if a little unused to such deference, but delighted by it just the same.

"I must apologise for my companions' lack of respect," she said, adding: "They are human you know," by way of explanation, placing a heavy emphasis on the word 'human.'

"Not at all Lady Celyn, not at all!" He chuckled. "It's perfectly fine. They have endured a great deal as I understand it, there will be time for all the usual pleasantries soon enough I'm sure."

The conversation between Celyn and the man in the paper crown gradually filtered through Liam, Evan and Travis's joviality, and they clambered to their feet, brushing away the coating of snow that was now covering their clothes.

"Evan, Liam," said Celyn, "I'd like you to meet the Lord of Misrule," indicating with an inclination of her head and a subtle but meaningful raising of her perfect eyebrows that they should bow.

Liam looked as if he was about to say something, but Evan, recognising from Celyn's deference to the strange man that he may be about to commit a major social gaffe, nudged him in the ribs. Liam thought better of any comment that he may have been considering. Despite their reservations, and no small degree of social discomfort due to the modern world's complete failure to prepare them for encounters with people with of this status, the brothers bowed towards the man who, in Celyn's world, was apparently royalty of some kind.

"Please, please rise," he said, gesturing wildly with his hands to urge them all to stand up. Evan and Liam stood up straight again.

Now that the initial elation of being reunited with Travis was beginning to subside a little, Evan and Liam gave voice to the questions they had been accumulating since their brother's disappearance.

"We thought you were gone forever. How on earth did you get away from the hunter?" asked Evan.

"Yeah, she went after you like a crazed zombie!" added Liam, referencing one of their preferred video games. "How did you manage to lose her?"

"I didn't," replied Travis. "She caught me." He held out his wrist to reveal deep purple and black bruising. For a moment Liam and Even were shocked into silence by the injury, so Travis continued: "I was running blind in the snow, I couldn't see where I was going, and eventually ran straight into a snow-dune. She was on me in seconds. But she would have caught me anyway. There was no way I was going to outrun a horse, and even if I could have, that dog would have got me, so in a way I suppose I was lucky that she reached me first."

"She must've grabbed you pretty bloody hard to bruise you like that," said Liam.

"Yeah, you're not wrong. It felt like a steel cable wrapped around my wrist, she was that strong, but the real damage was done when we left the ground. The pain was incredible; I was basically dragged into the air by my wrist. I thought my shoulder was going to be pulled out of its socket!"

Travis paused for a second and rubbed his shoulder.

"Go on then," urged Evan. "Tell us how you got away."

"That's the weird bit, I didn't really, I mean there was nothing I could do. I was swinging around by my wrist, dangling beside her horse, being pulled higher and higher into the air, when she just let go. At that point, I was sure I was going to die. I really had no idea of how high I was because of the snow, and the shock of being caught. For a moment, I couldn't even scream, it was like it was too much for my brain to process. I opened my mouth, but nothing happened. I think I did scream in the end, just as I hit a snow-dune. That was what saved me."

"So she was trying to kill you then?" asked Liam. "Dropping you like that."

"I don't think so. Something about it didn't feel deliberate. She didn't just suddenly drop me, it was more like she kind of forgot I was even there. Like I said, it was weird."

"So how did you find the Lord of Misrule then?" asked

Evan glancing over to Celyn as he spoke to check that he was using the title correctly.

"Well, that was just lucky, I suppose. I had sunk pretty deep into the snow-dune, and had the wind knocked out of me. I was flailing around in the middle of the dune trying to catch my breath, when suddenly a hand reached down and helped to pull me out," said Travis smiling over at the little man. The two had evidently established something of a bond in the time that Travis had been missing. The Lord of Misrule beamed back at him. "He pulled me out and helped me get away from the car park so that the huntress wouldn't find me if she came back."

"Well we clearly owe you a debt of gratitude for rescuing our companion your Lordship," said Celyn. "It is indeed very fortunate that you were nearby."

"Oh, not at all, please don't mention it," replied the Lord of Misrule. "But yes, it certainly was very fortunate that I happened to be taking a break from my duties, and was out enjoying the Solstice air, when I heard your young friend scream. Once he had informed me of the course of events that led to him being buried in a snow drift, I realised immediately that the Hunt was riding, and quickly made reparations by removing him to a place of safety. However, young Travis was most insistent that we should return to find you. He was very concerned that the Hunt might return to find the rest of you. And with good reason I'd wager, they don't give up easily!"

"And now you have heard my story, Lady Celyn, I would be most interested to learn what you have been up to this mid-winter's night that has brought the unwelcome attention of the Hunt upon you," he asked.

"Your Highness, we are engaged in a task that you may well find rather difficult to believe," she replied.

"Try me," he continued happily, "I am the Lord of Misrule," he said raising his arms dramatically to either side with a genial smile, "I'm sure I will have seen and heard stranger!"

"As you wish Your Majesty," began Celyn, and was about to elaborate when her eye was drawn to a subtle play of light that flickered for a fraction of a second against the slate wall of the photographic studio that bordered the right hand side of the alley way. Her brow furrowed slightly in confusion, and then smoothed out again so quickly that only someone looking directly at her would have noticed the brief change in her countenance. "We, uh, are just out looking for Liam's phone, that's what you called it isn't it Liam? He thinks he dropped it out here earlier."

"Wait, no I didn't," began Liam surprised at what had just been said, and then, noticing a slight widening of Celyn's eyes, continued with: "I, erm, dropped it in the town. It was when we were walking back through the car park that I realised it was gone"

"Well, whatever a 'phone' might be, I am sure it is not so valuable as to make it worth risking travelling any further towards town. As young Travis nearly found out to his cost, it can be perilous in the extreme to be abroad when the Hunt is riding. I would hate to think of any of you coming to any harm."

"I appreciate your advice your Lordship," said Celyn, "but humans have a special bond with phones, they are practically never apart, and to think of a phone lost and alone in the snow, bleeping pitifully for its owner causes them a great deal of distress. So you can appreciate that we really do need to continue our journey to town."

"Well, if you insist on proceeding," said The Lord of Misrule, "at least allow me to offer you a flagon of beer. No one should be without beer on the solstice!" This was an interesting turn of events for the brothers. Beer was a fairly recent discovery that was kept pretty well under control by their parents, and yet here was someone of obvious importance, who seemed to be insisting that they should partake. This, thought the brothers, was more like it! Despite his appearance, the Lord of Misrule was obviously a person of good taste and character.

"Well, thank you Your Majesty," said Celyn. "We would be honoured."

With a flourish, the man produced a foaming wooden mug of ale from somewhere within his robes and handed it to Celyn. She took a sip and passed it to each of the brothers in turn, warning each of them with a glance not to take too much. As they each put the mug to their lips in turn, the bubbles in the foaming head of the ale burst in their mouths, delivering a promise of the incredible taste that was to come. Then the beer flowed into their mouths, strong and dark and malty, a much deeper and richer flavour that anything they had encountered before, the taste alone was enough to make their heads spin. The temptation to keep drinking was almost overwhelming, but they had learnt to take heed of what Celyn said, and the alcohol seemed to go to their heads so quickly, that the surprise at their sudden light-headedness was enough to slow them down.

Evan, the last of the brothers to receive the mug, wiped foam from his mouth with a satisfied sigh as he returned it to Celyn.

"They are young, Your Majesty," said Celyn by way of an explanation for the short draught each had taken, "and not used to ale as fine as this, and we still have to find our way to the town," she continued passing the mug back.

"Well if you are sure, but I would be remiss in my duties if I didn't tell you that you are going completely the wrong way My Lady!" he said genially. "The town is in the other direction entirely. You should turn around immediately!"

Despite the fact that Liam's head was still spinning from the effects of the ale he had drunk, he nevertheless found a feeling of disappointment stealing through his mind to learn they were travelling in the wrong direction, until with a start he realised that since they had reached the alleyway they now knew exactly where they were. He glanced towards his brothers worried at this odd turn of events; this was clearly misinformation. Celyn however, smiled at the Lord of Misrule, seemingly unconcerned. In fact she appeared to be rather enjoying the deceit, as if it was all part of some game.

"Thank you kindly for the advice Your Majesty," she replied with a broad smile, "but I think we shall continue along this path. Unless, of course, that would cause you any offence," she added deferentially.

"Not at all my dear Lady Celyn," he said. "Not at all. Please proceed, but I fear you will have a wasted journey, you see, Travis and I were forced to skirt around the edge of the town as we hurried to put some distance between ourselves and any further encounter with that huntress, and I'm sorry to report that the whole of the town centre is blocked off by an impassable snow drift. I have never seen one so big. I do think you should reconsider."

Travis found himself nodding in agreement, as he recalled the monstrous piles of snow that the two of them had encountered on the outskirts of the town. In fact now he gave it some thought, it was almost as if they were back there again. The wall of drifted snow towered over them, its sheer glittering face reaching skyward so tall that as he looked up at it he became dizzy. The farther up the wall he looked, the dizzier he became until finally he had to reach out to steady himself. His outstretched hand encountered the wall of the alleyway, and his thoughts returned to the present, albeit somewhat sluggishly, thanks to the effect of the ale.

"Hang on a minute!" said Travis returning to his senses. "There was no snow drift. I mean there was snow, but nothing like you are talking about. What are you playing at? What's going on?"

"Oh very good, very good!" chuckled the Lord of Misrule. "Well done Travis! You soon saw through my little ruse. Have some more ale."

"You are very kind to offer my companions more ale', said Celyn, "But they really aren't used to beer as fine as this, so I think it is best if we regretfully decline."

"Of course, of course" he said taking back the mug, "Where are my manners? And now I must bid you farewell!" he said. "Solstice duties to perform, you know how it is!" And with that, he raced off across the car park in the direction they had come.

"What was all that about?" asked Evan.

"That," replied Celyn with a smile, "was all part of the fun of the Solstice. The Lord of Misrule is a very important participant in the solstice celebrations."

"The man in the shop mentioned the Lord of Misrule, but he said it was back in Roman times, two thousand years ago," said Evan.

"Maybe in your world," said Celyn, "but we aren't really in your world now. In my world the Lord of Misrule is very much of the present."

"Well," said Liam, with a smile and the taste of Otherworldly ale still in his mouth, "he seemed like a nicer guy than his title would suggest!"

"Well, strictly speaking, he's not really one person at all," Celyn explained. "Each solstice someone new is chosen to be the Lord, and they reign until the solstice has passed. They are in charge of the festivities and making sure that everyone has a good time, you know, ensuring that there is enough food for everyone, and that the beer flows freely. But a big part of their role is to turn all the normal rules on their heads: masters become servants, servants become masters, that kind of thing - hence the name. That is a big part of what makes the Solstice so special."

With the unexpected but pleasant distraction now apparently over, the group returned their attention to the task in hand and headed down the sloping alley-way that would lead them into the town.

18 FROST-FERNS

It was a simple task to navigate through the alley-way, bounded as it was along its entire length by walls so high that it was sheltered from most of the snowfall. This greatly aided visibility, but even without that advantage the walls were close enough together that both could be seen at once, even had the snow been falling as thickly as it was elsewhere. Another unexpected benefit of the proximity of the walls was that the group were able to steady themselves against them as they slipped and skidded down the steep icy slope.

Once he felt that they were far enough away from the Lord of Misrule that it would be safe to speak, Liam moved in next to Celyn as they walked along and asked:

"What was all that talk about lost phones Celyn? Is there some reason that you don't want the Lord of Misrule to know where we are going?"

"No, not at all," Celyn replied, "I'm not concerned about

the Lord of Misrule, he's completely harmless. No, for a moment I thought I saw something, I can't be sure though, but I certainly don't want to take any chances."

"Oh, ok," said Liam his voice quavering slightly. "Well is it something we should be worried about?"

"No, I don't think so," Celyn replied. "As I said, it may have been nothing."

With Liam reassured, they continued down the narrow passage. When they reached the bottom of the alley no one was really surprised to find that there was no snow drift as the Lord of Misrule had said there would be. But the brothers found that now they had an understanding of the Lord's role in the solstice celebrations, they were rather enjoying his misleading games. Despite this, it was difficult for them to suppress the little stab of fear they all felt, but none acknowledged, on exiting the reassuring confines of the narrow alley. Although they knew that Windsor Place lay before them, and no more than thirty feet away on the other side of the road lay a row of shops that would lead them to the town, all they could see was a disorientating, gently drifting wall of white.

Evan retrieved his smartphone from his pocket, launched the compass app, and waited for the digital needle to stop swinging and settle on North. He was pretty sure that the app did not need to do that, that it was perfectly well aware of in which direction North lay, and that it could have instantly directed him there without all the fancy graphics. However he was forced to acknowledge that he found this skeuomorphic behaviour oddly comforting, considering that the rest of the world seemed to be playing by a strange new set of rules, that it was apparently making up as it went along.

"Ok," he said, "the compass is ready. Let's go." And led the others out into the snow once more.

The eerie blue glow from the 'phone's display illuminated Evan's face from below, and as the only real source of light, further amplified their sense of isolation as it reflected back at them from the snowflakes all around, drawing them into their little bubble of light once more. With the aid of the compass app, it was not long before they encountered the blank wall of one of buildings on the far side of the road. However, it was still something of a surprise just how close they had to get before they could tell that there was anything there at all.

Turning to the left, the company followed the row of shops along, knowing that they would soon encounter another road cutting across their path. This next road would be Pondbridge Hill, a steep slope that would lead them all the way down to Fore Street, the location of the second-hand shop. They passed in front of another building and ventured once more out into the void as they crossed the open car parking space beside it.

"Right, this must be that little café," said Evan as he led them past the next building. "The next one will be the gift shop on the corner. We'll need to turn right down the hill after that."

When they reached what they assumed to be the gift shop on the corner of Windsor Place and Pondbridge Hill, Liam diverted in close to a window to try and peer in. Everything in this world was such a strange blend of the real and the fantastic that he was intensely curious as to what might be on display in the shop. He was soon disappointed when he realised that the glass was covered by thick frost-ferns that rendered it opaque. However as he looked closer, the swirling patterns within the ice revealed themselves to be worthy of further examination. At first he was mildly intrigued by the way that the impossibly complex ice crystals interlocked so perfectly, and how what little light there was slanted off each shard at a different angle, making the glass appear to jump and shift and flash from white to silver and back again as he moved his head. But when he focused his attention on a single 'frond', Liam noticed that the patterns seemed to spiral in on themselves in a way that seemed oddly familiar. As he looked closer, following the spirals around, he was amazed at the amount of intricate detail that he was able to make out. The shapes were similar to a Paisley design, but not quite - it was something else. He was briefly shaken out of his examination by the voice of one of his brothers.

"Come on Liam!" called Travis, from the rear of the group, as he realised that Liam had almost been left behind.

"Just a second," Liam replied, so fixated on the intricate swirling patterns on the glass that he didn't notice that Travis was the only member of the group who was still close enough to actually see him.

As he traced one of the entrancing whorls around with his fingertip, he noticed that the same pattern was repeated on a much smaller scale on one of the many little side spirals that were spawned at regular intervals from all along the edge of the main spiral. "Frost-fern is certainly a good name for these," he said to himself under his breath, the similarity between these icy patterns and living ferns was striking. Each of the smaller spirals looked to be a miniature replica of the main 'frond'. Then suddenly he realised what it was he had initially been reminded of: "Fractals!" he said out loud. "These look just like fractals." Liam had always had a natural talent for mathematics, and was familiar with the self-repeating nature of fractal patterns, in fact he had an idea he had even heard that frost crystals naturally displayed this phenomenon. But as he examined the pane of glass, so closely that his nose was almost in contact with the ice, he realised with a little jolt of surprise that these crystals bore a startling likeness to the fractal known as the "Julia Set". Actually, it was more than a similarity, the pattern was exactly the same as the Julia Set. Even weirder than this most recent discovery was that now that he was very close, it looked like the pattern was actually still developing as he watched! At the tip of each spiral, minute needles of ice were forming, continuing the whorl, and as they grew new spirals eddied off from them. The effect was disorientating, and he felt as though he was being drawn round and further into the pattern with each developing spiral.

Gradually he became aware of another force that seemed to be pulling in a different direction, urging him out of his spinning descent. Confused, Liam shook his head and looked up from the window and was surprised to find that Travis had his hand on his shoulder and was shaking him quite insistently, and that Celyn and Evan were also gathered around him.

"Take care Liam," warned Celyn. "It doesn't pay to allow yourself to become too absorbed in anything here."

"What? What do you mean?" asked Liam, shaking his head to try and clear it of the vagueness he seemed to be experiencing.

"You nearly got left behind, that's what," explained Evan, "We've been trying to call you away from this window for a couple of minutes now, but you just kept waving us away, and muttering about fractals and ferns and stuff. It was pretty scary to be honest."

"Really?" said Liam, clearly worried. He had no idea that he had been looking at the patterns for any more than a couple of seconds.

"Try not to worry about it. It's just the nature of this place," said Celyn. "Although it does seem to affect humans more than anyone else. You'll get used to it if you spend enough time here, and learn not to get drawn in."

"Now you mention it, the same thing happened to me in the town earlier," said Travis, and turning towards Evan added, "you remember, just before we got to the junk shop. You said I might be coming down with the 'flu or something."

"Yeah," said Evan, "but that was before it started snowing, so it can't have been anything to do with the Otherworld, can it?"

Freed from the strange attraction of the frost-ferns flowering across the gift shop window, Liam fell in behind Evan, while Travis and Celyn followed along behind. He was secretly relieved not to be at the back of the group as they turned to the right and set off down Pondbridge Hill.

Armed with renewed caution, the journey down the hill was slippery, but uneventful, and they soon moved into what in their world was Fore Street, the location of the old second-hand shop.

Travis looked around as they made their way along the road. It seemed to him as if the snowfall was lighter now, it was difficult to be sure though because the snow was falling so slowly that it was almost not moving at all, but he was sure that he could see through it further than he had been able to earlier. For one thing, he could dimly make out the fronts of the shops on either side of the road they were on, and it would not have been possible to see that far when they were crossing the car park.

19 REVELATION

As had been the case elsewhere when they had been sheltered by buildings, Liam, Evan, Travis, and Celyn's progress was relatively easy along Fore Street. The snow was still deep, and with each step they sunk up to their knees, but at least there were no snow-dunes blocking their path. With Evan still leading the way, they post-holed slowly along the road. Every window that they passed was etched with ferns as if an insomniac jeweller had been abroad in the night decorating each pane with an engraving tool; each one silvered and opaque and ethereally beautiful. Liam's experience meant that they were now all aware enough of the potential dangers able to be able marvel to at the effect without being drawn into its trap. As they moved along the road, the apparently weightless snow continued to swirl and eddy in their wake as they passed. This curious effect combined with the mysteriously obscured shop fronts leant a dreamlike quality to the dark and silent night.

When they eventually arrived at the second-hand shop, they were surprised to find the door standing open. A deep drift of snow flowed from the street down into the building.

"Look at the state of this place," said Evan looking through the open door at the snow-filled shop. "What a mess!"

He moved towards the door, and was just about to make his way inside when Liam called out to him: "Hang on a minute. Why's the door open? There could be anything in there."

"It's been forced. Look, the frame is split at the lock." said Travis ominously as he leaned past Evan to peer at the ruined doorframe.

Splinters of wood had been torn out of the doorframe where the lock engaged, the jagged edges of the freshly splintered wood strikingly white against the old dulled layers of paint that had been applied to the frame over many years.

Travis was surprised by the sharp scent of pine resin that emanated from the torn wood, still fresh despite the years that had passed since the tree was made into a door.

"I'm not sure this is a good idea," he said, something's forced the door open. It could still be inside for all we know."

"It's nothing," said Evan. "The weight of the snow has just forced it open. If anyone was in there we'd see their footprints wouldn't we. Come on, it'll be fine, we just need to get on with it."

Evan led the way, stooping under the lintel of the door which was now at eye-level thanks to the deep snow outside that had artificially raised the level of the street by several feet. One at a time they stumbled and slipped down the slope into the shop, each new arrival colliding with their predecessor when they reached the bottom. Even once they were inside, thanks to the open door, their breath still hung in thick clouds in front of them. The inside of the shop looked quite different from the brothers' last visit. The two worlds had blended so much now that the fixtures and fittings of the shop shimmered and swum before their eyes. Huge stalactites of ice hung from the ceiling, with smaller versions suspended from the overhanging edges of the various cupboards and counters in the shop, as clear and cold as ancient glaciers. In places the stalactites had fused with the stalagmites that had formed below them to form twisted columns of ice as thick as tree trunks, completely blocking access to some parts of the shop. A layer of snow covered every flat surface, and the air was unnaturally still. The bookcase was still in the same place, but its construction seemed to slowly flow from the planed wood that they were familiar with, to elaborate scrolls of dark metal highlighted with silver that was probably more usual in the Otherworld. Evan was the first to move towards it.

"Over here," he said. "We'd better get on with it."

They all moved to the bookcase and scanned the books that slowly drifted between states in the same way as the bookcase did. Initially fearful of touching things that seemed to belong to neither one world or the other, the brothers, following Celyn's lead, soon found that once they took hold of a book, it seemed to fix itself into one world.

Travis reached up and pulled a book from the shelf, dislodging a cascade of fine ice crystals, that flowed slowly earthwards at the same speed as the falling snow, rippling in the turbulence created by his arm as he lifted the book down.

They quickly scanned through the books looking for anything that they thought would be useful. Those that appeared to contain nothing of interest were returned to the icy bookshelves whilst anything that they thought might qualify they passed over to Celyn for closer examination.

Liam finished looking through his second book and placed it back on the bookshelf. He located a promising looking ancient leather-bound volume and reached up to the top shelf of the bookcase and took it down. He began to flick through the book, and was about halfway through, with his attention already beginning to wander as the images and text flashed past, when something on one of the pages that had just sped past nagged at him for attention. A picture on it seemed oddly familiar, but it had passed by so quickly that he couldn't be sure. He started flicking frantically backwards from the place he had stopped, muttering to himself so loudly that the others stopped what they were doing to look at him.

"What is it?" said Celyn, clearly interested in Liam's actions.

"Dunno," he said distractedly as he continued flipping pages. "Something just, dunno, something."

Suddenly he stopped. "Holy crap!" he said staring at the page.

"You're lucky Dad's not here to hear you say that," said Evan. "He'd go..." and then stopped, his comment left unfinished as he registered the expression on Liam's face.

Liam slowly lifted his gaze from the book to look at his companions. "You really need to see this," he said turning the open book around so the others could look at it. The book quivered as he held it out, partially because he was shivering, but mostly through shock.

"You may well be onto something with that," said Celyn looking at the page and talking in the voice she reserved for explaining Otherworldly matters to the brothers. "That is a Solstice blade, it's seriously powerful magic. Herla could certainly have used one to stop time, but it's highly unlikely. You see only a few were ever made, thousands of years ago, and none have been seen for almost as long. What was it that drew you to this particular image? You obviously haven't had much exposure to the Otherworld, so Solstice blades aren't something you would have come across before."

"I suppose it was something about the look of the thing," began Liam, "even in the drawing it just seems to radiate power." He paused for a second and then added: "That and the fact that Travis bought one as present for our mother in here earlier."

20 THE SOLSTICE BLADE

"What?" Exclaimed Celyn, as she looked in astonishment at the drawing of a solstice blade in the book that Liam was holding. "You have one of these? But that's impossible! Well, it's as good as impossible."

"That's definitely what we have," said Liam. "It wouldn't have stood out to me so much amongst all the other drawings otherwise, would it?"

"Yeah, he's right," said Travis. "No doubt about it. That's what I bought this evening."

"Well where is it then? Show me!" demanded Celyn.

"I can't show you it," replied Travis. "It's at home."

"At home," retorted Celyn. "Why in the world would you leave it there at a time like this?"

Even though he realised that Celyn had spoken before

having thought it through, Travis was embarrassed enough by her response to snap back at her: "How about because until two minutes ago it was nothing more than a paper knife I bought from a junk shop? How was I supposed to know it was some kind of magic artefact?"

"Yes, yes of course," replied Celyn, looking worried. "Look, please accept my apologies, I didn't think, and I'm sorry. But if you really do have a Solstice Blade," she continued, "then it is just possible that we could restart time. It won't be easy though, you've already seen some of what my world has in store. Are you sure you are prepared for this undertaking?"

"Well, we've got to do something," said Travis "whatever it takes, I'm in."

"Me too." added Liam.

"And me." said Evan.

"Well then," said Celyn. "In that case I'd better tell you what I know about Solstice Blades. To start with, they're ancient things. Even amongst my race, most people consider them to be little more than just bedtime stories for children."

"Because even though you live for so long the blades are older still?" said Liam. "Is that what you mean?"

"Exactly," replied Celyn, "and because they are so rare. If the stories are true, then only a few were ever made. Most of my own people don't really believe that they exist. In my world there are many things you as humans would have trouble believing in, yet I have never heard of anyone who has ever seen a Solstice Blade. That is why I was so surprised that you said you have found one."

"Ok then," said Liam, "so what else do we need to know?"

"Well, according to the legends, the blade is so sharp that it can cut through time, separating the solstice from the rest of the year, and thereby stop the solstice happening. But the reverse is also true; the same blade can be used to restore time again. So, if what you are correct and you really do have one, then we need to go and retrieve it, before someone else does."

"OK," said Travis, "so let's just get home and use it to restore time then."

"There is one other thing." said Celyn ominously.

"Well," said Evan impatiently "what is it?"

"In order to restore time, the blade requires a blood sacrifice." Now she really had their attention.

"Wait, what?" said Evan. "A blood sacrifice?"

Celyn could see that the brothers were worried about this, and continued: "It's not quite as bad as it sounds. Not much is needed, no one needs to be killed if that is what you are thinking, a single drop will do the trick. But it does have to come from the one who stopped the solstice in the first place."

"Just out of interest," said Liam, as a disturbing thought occurred to him, "how exactly is the blade used to stop the solstice?"

"In just the same way," said Celyn. "A blood sacrifice has to be made. Blood from a cut made by a solstice blade has to be dripped onto the earth."

"Just a drop?" asked Liam.

"Just a drop." replied Celyn.

"Then, I think know how all this happened," said Liam.

"Go on," said Celyn. "The more information we have the better if we are going to go up against the Wild Hunt."

"Well," began Liam, "It never snows here, so when it first started snowing earlier, we all went outside to mess around, you know, just throwing snowballs at each other and stuff. Anyway, after a while my hands started to go numb from the cold, so I went to get my gloves from my pocket, and when I did something cut me. When I looked at my hand to see what had happened, a drop of blood dripped onto the snow. Something weird definitely happened at that point - we all felt it. That pretty much sounds like what you said about how the solstice blade is used. But the strange thing is," he continued, "when I checked in my pocket, to see what had cut me there was nothing there; it was completely empty. And anyway, I am sure I left that knife on the coffee table in the front room when we went out. But then when we went back inside again after finding you it was gone; I'm sure of that, I looked everywhere."

"Well you didn't say anything about it," said Travis accusingly.

"Well, I wouldn't, would I?" replied Liam. "It was the

present you had bought for mum, and I thought I'd lost it; and anyway, we had other things on our minds," he said, inclining his head towards Celyn.

"It must have been a Solstice Blade that cut you," said Celyn. "It's all too much of a coincidence not to be. Somehow someone was able to get that blade into your pocket." Celyn could see that Liam was quite concerned now, and she continued reassuringly, "Don't feel bad about it, it's not your fault," she said. "The blade is not of this world. It should never have been here in the first place."

As she was talking, Celyn became aware of a rhythmic tapping sound apparently coming from somewhere within the shop. The insistent nature of the noise made it rather irritating and distracting. She stopped talking and tilted her head to one side briefly to try and locate it, but after a few seconds more the sound stopped. Dismissing it as probably the beams and joists of the old shop creaking and complaining about the cold she continued:

"The situation was beyond your control. The people behind this knew exactly what the blade was and what it could do. You were being manipulated, but there is no way you could have known it. I suspect that King Herla is deeply involved, but he can't have done this alone - he must have had help."

"He seemed like a man who is pretty capable of getting what he wants, earlier," Evan pointed out.

"True," said Celyn in reply. "But don't forget that he is unable to walk on the earth, and that's a pretty severe restriction."

"But where could it be now?" asked Liam. "I just said that when I checked my pocket there was nothing there. Take a look for yourself if you like; I'm still wearing the same coat."

"My best guess is that it fell out of your pocket when you pulled your hand out after cutting yourself," said Celyn. "It would have sunk straight into the snow, and any trace of it would soon have been covered up by more; so it's unlikely you would have noticed it. I think, in all probability, it is still out there now. All we need to do is get back there and find it," and then, as the tapping noise started up again, she added: "Can't anyone else hear that?" The sound was irritating her more than it should have done, but she couldn't work out why that was.

Unconcerned by Celyn's growing annoyance, Travis spoke up "It's nothing, just the joists creaking. But look, won't the hunt be searching for it as well though? I mean they won't want to run the risk of us re-starting the solstice, will they?"

"Unlikely," said Celyn. "For one thing, they don't think we even know what it is. King Herla probably didn't think any further ahead than getting one of you to cut yourselves, why would he? You couldn't have known the blade's purpose, or what to do with it, and anyway, he knew it would have soon been covered up by the snow."

"And that is our next problem," said Evan. "if it's under the snow how are we ever going to find it again?"

"We have this," replied Celyn, tapping her index finger against her holly pendant. "If we can get near enough to it, that blade is going to light up like a beacon!"

All the time she had been talking, the knocking noise had continued its maddening rhythm. Finally it became too much for her to tolerate any longer. "What in the world is that noise?" she shouted.

"Yeah, I was wondering that too" said Evan, "I don't think it is the joists. It's been going on too long for that. It seems to be coming from over there," nodding towards the rear of the shop.

"Knockers!" yelled Celyn.

"What?" said Travis, an amusing reply already starting to form in his mind in response to what he interpreted as a semi-rude word. He did not finish his thought though, because at that point, the old shop exploded into action, as everything seemed to happen at once.

Celyn was on the move, racing across the floor in the direction indicated by Evan.

Apparently in reaction to Celyn's movement, a chest of drawers at the back of the shop tipped violently forward, its drawers sliding out as it fell, and crashed to the ground. The items piled up on top of it scattered and rolled across the floor, slowing down as they moved away from the group and fell under the influence of the alternate time-scale of the solstice.

At the same time, a creature, the size of a child of three or four, flew out from behind the upturned chest of drawers and ran towards the door. As it raced past Travis, he stared open mouthed in surprise as he got a clear look at it. Its head was large compared to the size of its body, with eyes that were even more out of proportion; much larger than expected. Flapping either side of its head as it ran, were large bat-like ears, but the most bizarre aspect of its appearance was the chameleon-like camouflage that flowed across its skin. Patches of bright light chased dark shadows across a background of jagged browns and greens. It looked exactly like candle light on uneven rock.

Celyn reacted by scooping up a heavy - sometimes wooden, sometimes silver - candle holder from the floor as she turned to face the door, and hurled it towards the fleeing creature. The candle holder never really stood much chance of hitting its target as it stuttered through different time lines, it's speed alternating between fast and slow, before eventually smashing through a large glass bottle standing just beside the door, showering the area with broken glass, just as the creature ran up the ramp of drifted snow and swerved out of the door into the snow-covered street.

21 AURORA

Liam, Evan and Travis stood open-mouthed in shock and surprise, as they mentally processed the events that had just unfolded. Evan was the first to recover: "What on earth was that?" he asked.

"I'll explain on the way," said Celyn, with an urgent tone in her voice. "But the first thing we need to do is move, and fast!" And with that she gathered up her skirts and started to struggle up the slope of drifted snow that had spilled down through the open door of the shop. As each footstep crunched down through the snow, little powdery avalanches flowed back down the incline into the shop. The brothers were quick to follow her, stumbling up the snow drift. By the time they had climbed about halfway up, they were able to reach forward and grab hold of the doorframe and haul themselves up the remainder of the slope, ducking under the unexpectedly low lintel and out into the street.

Outside, the group followed the trail left by the fleeing creature back along Fore Street. It was difficult for them to attain any real speed, as their legs sank deeply into the snow with each step, and the effort of hauling themselves free again only to repeat the whole process as soon as they put the next foot down, quickly drained them of their energy. During the time that they had been in the second-hand shop, the snowfall had almost completely abated; now only an occasional flake hung almost motionless in the air. Without the dense snow obscuring anything more than an arm span away, the fronts of the shops on either side of the street were now clearly visible to the group. Although dunes of snow piled up against them still partially obscured the windows. As he laboured along the street, Travis gradually became aware of the soft glow of bands of colour drifting gently across the surface of the snow, and he too looked upwards to try and locate the source of the illumination. It didn't take him long. Above them the sky was aflame. The wavering curtains of coloured light of a spectacular aurora rippled across the narrow band of sky between the two opposing rows of shops. For a few seconds the brothers stood and gazed upward, transfixed. Evan noticed that if he focussed hard on the spectacle, it would occasionally resolve into the coloured lights of the town's Christmas decorations that had been strung between shop fronts. Evidently they weren't completely in the Otherworld just yet, but artefacts of their own world were becoming less and less common.

"Come on," said Celyn eventually, spurring the group into motion again. "We really don't have time to appreciate the view. We've still got a Solstice Blade to find."

As they post-holed their way along the road, she tried to explain the events of the previous few minutes in the shop.

"Based on what just happened," said Celyn between heavy breaths, "I'm going to guess that we are in the place you call

Cornwall, is that right?"

"Yes," answered Evan, his head enveloped in thick white clouds with each breath, "this is Cornwall. What difference does that make? There's nothing special about Cornwall."

"Depends on your perspective," continued Celyn. "Our two worlds naturally lie closer together in certain places, and Cornwall is one of them. It is easier for my people to enter your world and vice versa in places like Cornwall than it is elsewhere. You must have heard legends and stories of people who get lost and accidentally slip through into another realm."

"Yeah, I think so," said Evan.

"Well, when that happens, it is generally in places like this, so, depending upon your point of view, I'd say that Cornwall is pretty special."

"Ok," said Evan. "I get what you mean, and that might explain why any of this is happening at all. But you would have come to that conclusion before. What is it about what just happened that made you think that you were in Cornwall?"

"That creature in the shop was a knocker," she explained.

"I've heard of knockers!" said Travis.

"Yes, I bet you have," retorted Evan, between deep lungfuls of freezing air as he continued trudging through the snow, fairly certain he knew where this was headed. "But in case you haven't noticed by now, this is serious!"

"No, really," continued Travis, his speech punctuated with sounds of exertion, "I'm sure we learned about them when we were still in junior school. You remember! We did a project about the myths and legends of Cornwall. Weren't knockers spirits that lived in the old mines?"

"Yes that's pretty much it." replied Celyn, "Hundreds of your years ago they used to knock on the walls of the mines to guide the miners to veins of tin and copper. That of course is how they got their name. The presence of the knockers in the mines was a fortunate consequence of the proximity of our two worlds to the miners - although of course they didn't know it. To them, the knockers were simply benevolent mine spirits, but relations between the knockers and human miners were good for hundreds of years."

Celyn's heavy velvet skirt was making her progress along the shopping street much more laborious than it was for her companions, and as they reached the junction of Fore Street with Pondbridge Hill, she stopped to catch her breath. Above their heads the aurora still shimmered and rippled across the sky like a wind-blown flag.

After a few rasping, laboured breaths, Celyn felt recovered enough to continue with her explanation. "The knockers took great pride in guiding their human counterparts to the best veins of ore. Eventually though, as you know, the mines began to close down. Of course, to the miners, this was a gradual process, but to the knockers who lived in the timescape of the Otherworld, it felt like the miners left overnight. Eventually, most of the knockers came to understand what had happened and adapted, but some of them felt slighted and abandoned by the humans, and over time, that sense of abandonment grew into a desire for revenge. I suspect that our friend from the old shop is one of those who were unable to adapt. I also suspect that the purpose of his knocking was to guide the Wild Hunt straight to us, and that is why we have to move quickly. If he gets word to the hunt that we know about the role of the solstice blade in all this, they are obviously going to try and stop us recovering it."

Having recovered a little, they began the ascent of Pondbridge Hill. Now that the snow had stopped falling, they found that navigation was much easier, and they were able to see to the top of the hill quite clearly. The steep slope led up to the main road through the town, and on the other side lay the alley back up to the cattle market car park. As it happened, the majority of the snow seemed to have accumulated at the bottom of the incline, so their progress was actually a little easier than it had been along Fore Street. In every direction that they looked the town appeared very different. Enormous drifts and banks of snow obscured most of the fronts of the buildings, and large icicles hung threateningly from those parts that were still exposed. Occasionally a sharp cracking sound reverberated around the otherwise silent streets, making the group look around anxiously, as one or another of the giant icicles threatened to let go, and slam down into the snow. The brothers looked around them as they continued up the hill. Oddly those portions of shop signs that they could see made no sense, and appeared to be written not only in a foreign language, but also in an unknown alphabet. The disorientating and uncomfortable shifting of objects between the two worlds that had been most evident in the shop had all but stopped now. Their immersion into Celyn's world felt almost complete, and by now the aurora refused to reveal its Christmas light origins to even the most concentrated stare. This and the many other distractions meant that it seemed like no time at all had passed before the group found themselves across the road and beginning their ascent up through the alleyway where they had met the Lord of Misrule earlier, and they soon stumbled out of the other end into the car park.

The aurora was now falling behind them, and through the clear air the other end of the car park was plainly visible. As they crossed the snowfield, their path was criss-crossed by tracks left by animals and the footprints of other small, apparently humanlike, creatures. The snow dunes piled up around them had been sculpted into unusual shapes by the winds of earlier, so it appeared almost as if they were traversing a frozen sea. Starlight sparkled off a million facets in hard cold pinpricks of light as they moved. Occasionally, in the distance, other lights twinkled on and off in the snow, whether from other travellers across the snow, or from the windows of strange Otherworldly dwellings, they could not tell. Now that they were able to see their route, and they no longer had to rely on the compass, it didn't take long for the group to cross the expanse of snow. They reached the ramp at the other end of the car park and skidded and slipped down back on to the lane that they had earlier had to navigate by following the high stone wall along its edge.

22 KNOWLEDGE

The knocker spoke in excited breathless bursts, as agitated flashes of light raced across his skin, brightly enough to illuminate the nearest walls of the cavern.

"They know about the blade!" he spluttered urgently. "I had to run all the way here."

"What? But they can't!" echoed the reply. "Even in the Otherworld no one believes in Solstice Blades."

"Well they do! And they almost caught me. She threw a candle-stick at me!"

"Ok, just calm down and tell me what they know."

The knocker closed his eyes for a second and the rapid flashes of light coursing madly across his body slowed to a gentle flicker.

"They found a picture in a book. One of the humans

recognised it as the blade they bought earlier, the one we planted there, and then she figured out the rest. They are travelling back to the house now."

"Ok, ok, it's bad news, but it's not too bad, we don't need to worry too much just yet, they may know what the blade is, but they'll never find it, it was lost in the snow."

"Oh, they will, they will!" replied the knocker, as little splashes of light began to dance over his skin again. "She has the necklace. The blade shouldn't be here, and the necklace knows it - it will show it up!"

In the dark something smashed and splintered against the wall of the cavern with a hollow crack.

"Damn her! I'll make sure she regrets sabotaging my plans! Go and summon the Hunt, we might as well put those idiots to some good use. They got us into this situation by giving into their base instincts in the first place, so they can use them to get us out of it again."

The knocker's anxious display of illumination subsided to be replaced with a delighted glow that spread gradually across his shoulders and up his neck into his head before finally flowing out along his ears.

"Yes, yes," he said happily, "the Hunt will see to them."

Silence and darkness returned to the cavern.

23 OTHERWORLD

When the group arrived back in the garden, or more precisely where the garden would have been in their world, it was clear for them to see how they had become lost so easily earlier in the day. Now, with the benefit of snow free skies, the three brothers looked out over a world that was vastly different from the one they were used to seeing from their back garden. With the solstice almost upon them, their immersion into Celyn's world was complete. The blurring of the two domains that they had experienced in the town was not in evidence at all. From the top of the hill where their garden used to be, the snow covered land fell away unobstructed by garden fences, buildings, telegraph poles, and walls, down to a broad wooded valley far below. The rows of houses that they should have seen beyond the fence at the bottom of the garden were gone, leaving only the snowy slope which ascended again in the distance to barren moorland, empty, except for clusters of twinkling lights indicating the locations of scattered settlements. To the south, the few isolated areas of woodland that existed in our world, had merged to become a great forest. Above the whole vista curved the great arc of the sky, deepest indigo and blazing with the light of a billion stars. Just above the horizon to the west, and bathing the whole incredible scene below in soft light, hung the moon of the Otherworld, huge and low and yellow.

Liam, Evan and Travis stood stunned, and gazed out over the transformed world beyond their back door.

"Come on," said Celyn. "We don't have any time to waste. We have just one chance to retrieve the solstice blade. If the Hunt gets to it first, we are lost."

Celyn held out the holly necklace once more, and immediately a point of light blinked into existence far out in the woods at the bottom of the slope.

"Well it looks like your theory was right Liam," said Travis. "The blade must have been in your pocket, it must have been that that cut you."

"But it's so far away," said Liam, shocked at the distance they had strayed from the house in the snowstorm, and amazed that they had ever managed to find their way back. "We were just in the back garden when I dropped the knife."

"Time and distance are not the same in the Otherworld," said Celyn. "When you dropped the blade in your world you were right here. In my world you were way over there. At another time it would have ended up somewhere else."

"Well, in that case, we'd better get moving then hadn't we?" said Travis, directing his remark towards Evan, whose life-long interest in astronomy was currently overriding his more recently discovered interest in restoring time and returning to his own world.

Evan gazed upwards: "Oh, wow! Have you seen this?" he said. "It's incredible!" Above them arching across the night sky from horizon to horizon was the spiral arm of the Galaxy. But this was no faint Milky Way; despite the glare of the full moon, the Galaxy above them glowed with light. Even the dark dust clouds that obscured some of the star fields were illuminated in reds and violets and blues. Looking at it was like watching the gears of the universe slowly turning. Further out in space, the brothers could make out more distant galaxies in startling detail with the unaided eye. The spectacle seemed to have little respect for conventional time, as they watched stars being born in towering stellar nurseries, and flowering into supernovae in the space of an instant. Spinning galaxies collided, dragging out faint tails of stars deep into the night as they watched. The scene was intoxicating and Evan stared upwards, entranced as the universe revolved above him while the world turned beneath his feet.

A soft hand on his shoulder dragged him back to the present. "It's rather overpowering the first time you see it isn't it?" said Celyn gently. "Few other humans have seen what you are seeing now, but I'm sorry to say that you do eventually get used to it." Evan drew his gaze back from the living heavens and looked at her. He seriously doubted that he ever would.

"We really do have to go now," said Celyn. "They'll be here soon." As if on cue the distant sound of shouting and the baying of hounds reached their ears. It was far enough away that they felt they were in no immediate danger, but they knew that the feeling of safety wasn't going to last for long.

The company made their way, slipping and stumbling,

down the hill towards the point of light that marked where the solstice blade lay buried in the snow. As they descended they left deep trails behind them, dotted with deeper pits where their feet had sunk in. Walking was tiring: every few steps, once their feet had sunk down, the support promised by the newly compressed snow beneath them would prove to be an illusion, and they would suddenly jolt down even deeper. The constant creaking sound of the snow compacting beneath their feet that at first had been new and interesting was now beginning to become very tiresome.

Just as they were nearing the bottom of the hill, but still only about a third of the way to where the glowing patch of snow indicated the location of the blade, the unmistakable sound of the peculiar frequency spanning calls of the Wild Hunt caused them to stop in shock.

"Bloody hell! That sounds close!" said Travis. "I thought they'd still be miles away."

"We're being slowed down by the snow," said Liam. "And don't forget they were guided straight to us by that knocker. Once they knew that we were in the town, all they would've needed to do was follow our trail."

Any further explanation that Liam may have been planning on was abandoned as Celyn suddenly called out in panic: "Run!" The urgency in her voice sent a tidal bore of adrenaline surging through their blood vessels, and gave them the energy they needed to launch themselves out of the snow and half run half lope down to the bottom of the hill. Once they were off the slope, the four of them raced as best they could across the valley floor, the deep snow forcing them to take unnaturally high steps to lift their tired legs out of the snow, only to sink in again up to their knees each time they put a foot down. But at least they were closing in on the solstice blade. They could now make out that the point of light they had seen from the top of the hill was a bright glow apparently originating underneath the snow in the trees ahead of them

"Keep going!" shouted Celyn between obviously painful breaths, noticing that their pace was beginning to slow again. The brothers complied without answering, all of their energy was needed to just keep moving. By now they were less than one hundred feet from where the blade lay, but the sounds of the hunt were very close.

At seventy five feet from the blade, their energy was almost completely spent.

Trying to keep moving was like trying to run in a dream; huge amounts of effort were required to make very little progress. In desperation, each of them reached forward grabbing handfuls of snow, vainly hoping for some purchase to allow them to pull themselves forward. But the treacherous snow crumbled in their grip, taking their energy and giving nothing back.

Fifty feet:

A deeper drift of snow grabbed at Liam's legs and caused him to stumble. Travis grabbed his arm as he fell and yanked him back on to his feet. Behind them, the sound of the hunt had swelled to a cacophony of blaring horns, yelping, barking, shouting and whinnying.

Twenty five feet:

Thundering hooves shook the ground beneath them with a

sound like hell's own freight train clattering out of control towards them.

Ten feet:

Hot breath on their necks. Snarling that was no longer perceived as a general threat somewhere behind them, but identifiable by their adrenaline drenched brains as individual hunting hounds to the left and right.

Five feet:

Unbearable noise and fear. Claws, snagging on clothing, barely snatched free.

Then they were upon them.

The hunt screamed overhead, the whole of the Otherworld shaking in protest as they tore a hole through the night. With the last of his strength, Liam threw himself forward into the snow, as snarling jaws ripped through the air inches above him. His mind registered snatched images of wet sweat-soaked fur as it flew over him in a mad blur; the animal stench causing him to screw his face up. Evan did the same, his teeth gritted as the noise threatened to shake them free of his jaw, as his face slammed into the cold snow. Travis and Celyn were a few feet ahead of the others with Celyn in the lead. She was almost at the blade when the hunt shrieked over them. Travis looked on in numb shock as a heavily muscled arm wreathed in tattered rags reached down and swept Celyn up into the air.

As the rider who had taken Celyn ascended rapidly into the sky, he swung her up behind him as if she weighed nothing, and in one movement dumped her on to the saddle behind him. Celyn had no choice other than to wrap her arms around him and cling on. Almost immediately, one of the other riders urged his mount skywards as well, rapidly closed in on them and reached across and snatched the holly pendant away from her neck. Travis numbly noted the broken necklace coiling through the air as it fell earthward. The glow in the snow indicating the location of the solstice blade abruptly snapped out.

"Get the blade!" screamed Celyn as loudly as she could, just before her voice became lost in noise of the hunt.

In the final moment of the Wild Hunt's passage overhead Travis launched himself at the point where, until a split second ago, the light had been. His upward movement caused him to connect with the wildly flailing hoof of one of the horses, and everything went black as he was flipped over in the air and smashed down onto his back into the snow.

24 SOLSTICE

Like a swimmer returning to the surface after a dive to the bottom of a pool, Travis gradually became aware of noise around him. At first it was muffled and indistinct, but it rapidly became louder, and as consciousness returned he was able distinguish that it was coming from different directions. The next thing he became aware of was the fact that a strand of hair was sticking his cheek. He brushed it away, and was surprised to find that it wasn't hair but water. Still trying to make sense of where he was and what was happening, he looked down at his hand to discover that it was streaked with blood. He touched his head again; the source of the blood seemed to fit in with a pounding headache that was just beginning to make its presence known. Travis shook his head to try and clear his mind, and quickly regretted it. The disjointed, swimming images filling his vision gradually resolved themselves into a gathering of huge black horses, nostrils flaring from exertion, snorting and tossing their heads irritatedly. Seated atop the horses and tugging on their bridles to keep them in line as they pranced and stamped were the hunters: wild-eyed from the chase, and dressed in rags, they were gaunt and lined but well muscled. In the centre, and marked as the leader of the fearsome group by a wickedly pointed tarnished crown that must once have been gold, but was now mostly burned black by a hundred lightning strikes, sat the tallest of the group. Packs of hunting hounds were arrayed on either side of the horses and kept in place by long leather tethers held by some of the horsemen.

The leader looked over to one the horseman holding on to the hounds, and with a tilt of his head indicated that he should approach Travis. The rider kicked his heels into the horse's side, and urged it toward Travis. The hounds started to bark and yap in excitement as they detected the movement of the horse, and pulled ahead, straining at their leashes to try to get closer to Travis. Still lying on the ground with the wind knocked out of him by the impact, fear began to course through Travis's body. As the hounds moved closer, he tried to kick away from them with his feet, but they could find no purchase in the deep snow. Even though there was clearly no escape, instinct forced Travis to try and stand up. Still kicking wildly, he planted his hands on to the freezing snow and tried to push himself up from his position lying on his back. He managed to raise himself up just a little, but the snow gave way beneath his hands, and he fell back again, plunging his hands deeper into the snow up to his elbows. The hounds edged forward until they were close enough to Travis that he could feel their hot breath on him, drops of saliva sprayed his face as they bayed in a frenzy at the end of their leashes.

In desperation, Travis tried to force himself up again, but this time, as he pushed down with his hands, instead of numbing snow, on his left side he felt cold hard metal. Instinctively, his fingers closed around the buried knife, and he rolled himself violently on to his right side. His arm exploded through the snow. Holding the solstice blade before him he screamed "Keep away! Keep your bloody dogs away!"

To his surprise, the dogs were startled by his sudden outburst; either that, or they were affected by the sudden and unexpected appearance of the solstice blade, because they immediately slunk backwards a few feet snarling and snapping at the air in front of them. Travis's relief was short lived however as the figure in the tarnished crown took an immediate and unwelcome interest in him. The leader of the hunt leaned menacingly forward in the saddle, looked directly at Travis and spoke in a growling voice that carried within it echoes of the howling wind.

"The blade."

The creature's voice was both commanding and terrifying; and Travis, incapacitated by fear, felt compelled to obey, when suddenly another voice shouted from within the group.

"Don't give it to him," instructed Celyn from deep within the group. "Remember they can't dismount!"

Travis felt the familiar disorientation that accompanied Celyn's use of her influence. The recognition helped him to realise that the leader of the hunt had the same ability, and that understanding gave him a little power to resist it.

"She's right," shouted Liam from where he had landed in the snow a short distance away. "He can't take it from you if he can't dismount. All he can do is try and coerce you into giving it to him."

"Perhaps not," came yet another voice, "but I can!"

The horses parted to reveal a man, barely two feet tall and dressed in mismatched and colourfully patched clothes. On his head he wore a crumpled purple paper crown. Despite his strange appearance he radiated malevolence, and Liam, Evan and Travis recognised him immediately.

"Your Majesty?" said Travis, confusion evident in his voice. "What, what are you doing here?" he continued as struggled to process this new information.

"Shut up and give me the blade," said the Lord of Misrule bluntly.

Travis was stung. This was someone that he counted as a friend. He glanced over to where Liam and Evan stood, their mouths open in bewilderment, they looked as shocked as he was. "But, but you rescued me from that hunter, you helped me find Celyn and my brothers again," he said, not really expecting a reply, just hoping that expressing his jumbled thoughts would help make sense of them. "You gave us ale."

"The only reason I rescued you from the hunt to stop you going into town to find that book. If they hadn't been chasing you, you never would have left your house. Those idiots practically drove you to the only way there is to undo all my work. I told you shouldn't attribute too much intelligence to the hunt," he said with bristling resentment.

Travis looked nervously towards the huge hunter in the corroded crown, expecting an explosion of rage to be directed at the Lord of Misrule for this insult. If he was angered, he didn't show it. The hunt seemed to defer to the Lord of Misrule as much as Celyn had. His authority over the solstice appeared to be absolute.

Then Celyn's voice called out from somewhere within the ranks of hunters: "The Lord of Misrule! It was all him all along. He's the one you've..." but her voice was abruptly cut off. Travis felt sick at the thought that Celyn might have been hurt, but acknowledged that he had heard her with a slight nod of the head just in case she could still see him. Travis understood: the Lord of Misrule had started all this, and he was the one whose blood would be needed to restart the solstice. In the time it took to form the thought the man in the paper crown was almost upon him.

Travis braced himself for the struggle that was surely to follow, when he sensed a sudden change in the world. He wasn't the only one to have noticed. The horses which had been becoming progressively more agitated stopped stamping, and the hounds fell silent. The huntsmen sniffed the air and cocked their heads to the right and left as if searching for the source of some expected, but as yet unheard, sound. The nature of time seemed to change as the next few seconds passed by in a flash, but also seemed to slow to a crawl so that Liam, Evan and Travis were able to process every piece of new information as if it were all happening at half speed. As the brothers looked on in bewilderment, the air seemed to crystallise around them. The soft currents of night breeze seemed to take on solid form, and blurred and flowed around them. The night itself took on a fragile, brittle quality as if any errant event had the potential to send the world spinning down some new path.

The Lord of Misrule laughed, threw his crowned head backwards and shouted triumphantly. "The solstice is upon us! You are too late!" then turning back to Travis he said: "Now, give me the blade."

Travis knew that this was their only chance. Quickly, he glanced over to his left then his right, catching the eye of Liam and then Evan and an unspoken understanding passed between them. Because, when it comes down to it, although the brothers might fight and bicker and not get on sometimes, their fifteen years together were worth a lifetime in adult years, and they knew each other's thoughts better than anyone in any world. Travis looked at Liam and Liam knew, he looked at Evan, and Evan knew. Then Travis looked at the Lord of Misrule, he might have the whole Wild Hunt behind him, but they had crossed a line when they took Celyn.

As the little man in the paper crown reached towards him, Travis raised his arms up in front of his face in defence. The Lord of Misrule chuckled in satisfaction and reached for the blade in Travis's left hand, but as he did so, with a dramatic wave of his hand, Travis switched the blade from his left hand to his right. A brief flicker of confusion passed across the Lord of Misrule's face as he registered Travis's elaborate flourish, but unperturbed he lurched to the right and grasped the hand containing the paper knife. Even though he was expecting this, Travis was shocked by the power of the little man, and despite using all his strength, could not resist as his fingers were slowly forced open. His hand shook violently as he used all of his strength attempting to resist;, but agonisingly slowly, the Lord of Misrule managed to peel open finger after finger, until finally Travis could resist no longer, and his hand fell open to reveal nothing at all.

"What?" screamed the Lord of Misrule enraged.

Travis winked at him, and said: "Misdirection. Classic conjurer's trick - you never lose it!" and then he flung his left hand out towards Liam. The solstice blade slid out from where he had dropped it down into the left sleeve of his jacket during the apparent switch to his right hand. The knife flew across the gap to Liam, tumbling, end over end, through the frozen air, first the lethally sharp blade pointing straight at him, and then the carved handle.

In the curiously distorted time of the solstice, Liam was able to see every twist and turn of the knife as if it was in slow motion as it flashed straight towards him. Judging the moment to perfection, he bought his foot up in an explosion of snow, and connected with the knife in an aerial scissor kick, immediately sending it sailing back towards the Lord of Misrule and Evan who was standing beyond him. The Lord of Misrule was still reacting to the surprise appearance of the blade when he found that it was now flying straight back at him. Just as his head turned to look towards Liam, the solstice blade flashed past his ear, slicing through the very tip as it passed, and trailing a thin streamer of bright red blood in its wake that seemed to float gracefully on the air. Again, the brothers were able to discern every detail of the events despite the speed at which it was all happening. As the Lord of Misrule raised his hand to his ear, and let out a little yelp of pain, the tiny ribbon of blood coalesced into a few quivering drops as bright as holly berries, and began to fall down to the snow.

The knife was still on an ascending path, as Evan summoned every last ounce of strength and launched himself upwards out of the snow. With supernatural timing, enhanced by the curious effects of the solstice, he stretched up with his right hand and snatched the blade right out of the air. As he fell backwards towards the snow, he twisted like a cat to ensure that he would not land on his back. He was only going to have one chance to get this right. Feet first, he plunged straight through the covering of snow, slamming into the ground beneath so hard that his knees buckled under him. The whole world seemed to hold its breath as he managed to regain his balance, the solstice blade glinting in the light of the big yellow moon above him in his outstretched hand. At its tip was a single drop of blood.

By now the Lord of Misrule was on his feet and rushing Evan in a final desperate attempt to stop him, but Evan's mind was racing. With a wry smile at the Lord of Misrule, he bought his arm down with lightning speed and plunged the solstice blade through the snow and deep into the ground.

25 TIME

The instant the blade hit the ground, a deep rumbling, grinding sound shook the earth on which they were standing as if the stalled machinery of the universe had lurched back into motion. Along with the juddering that reverberated through the ground beneath their feet, the world around them swum and twisted in their vision for a few endless seconds as the world we know and the Otherworld began to tear apart from each other. The rumbling in the earth increased in intensity, becoming louder and louder until it was a subsonic wave that crashed through the ground, churning the earth as if it was water. The vibrations threatened to throw them all off their feet, and the brothers staggered as they struggled to retain their footing. The Wild Hunt's horses stamped and reared up on their hind legs, frightened by the way the ground moved like liquid beneath them. The hounds cowered and shook with their tails curled beneath them in fear, but if they were howling or whining, no one could hear. Soon the mad, unnatural distortions in the air became so intense that Liam, Evan and Travis were forced to screw their eyes closed. All the while, the noise continued to increase in volume until it became too painful to endure, and they had no option but to cover their ears.

Then, instantly, it was gone, and just as when the solstice blade first drew blood earlier in the evening, everyone present felt that some fundamental change in the nature of things had occurred: this time it felt like loss.

After the violence and noise of the two worlds separating, the world suddenly seemed very quiet. For a moment, it felt as if they all inhabited a void, a desolate, empty place. The one remaining thing was a small sound, a quiet whining that slowly grew in intensity to a sobbing wail.

"No, no, no, no, no!" cried the Lord of Misrule.

The brothers cautiously opened their eyes.

King Herla looked over to him. "It's over," he said simply.

"But it can't be!" Exclaimed the Lord of Misrule, who looked rather less menacing now, and much more like the character they had first encountered in the car park. "It was all so perfect: the plan, it was perfect. How can it have failed?"

"The solstice has passed. Let it go," said Herla.

"But you ..." began the little man in the tattered paper crown, "you can't just give up. We were so close! How can you just accept this?"

But he already knew that it was too late. Herla was right; the solstice had passed, but something else had changed as well. The Lord of Misrule could see it in every member of the hunt as he looked from one rider to another. The wildness was gone from their eyes, and had been replaced with something else. Something like longing, something like acceptance.

"Now just wait a minute," began the Lord of Misrule as he desperately looked from face to face with increasing agitation, but before he could continue, a disturbance rippled through the ranks of the hunt from somewhere towards the middle of the group. One of the riders had shifted position in their saddle in way that seemed out of place. Instinctively, with subtle movements of their legs and twitches of their reins the closest members of the group coaxed their mounts away. Within a few seconds a lone rider was left in the centre of a clear circle at least twenty feet across.

"Look," said Liam to Evan pointing at the rider. "That's the one that took Travis.

As they watched, the huntress gazed around her with eyes that were clear, bright and wide open in recognition, with none of the confusion that plagued her earlier in the evening. She sat up tall on her horse, as she calmly began to wind the reins around the pommel of her saddle. This action appeared to deeply unsettle the rest of the hunt, as several of the horses began to toss the heads tried to turn in circles as their riders fought for control.

"Chastity, hold!" instructed Herla, a note of alarm clearly audible in his tone.

But the horsewoman merely looked in his direction and smiled: "Don't take on so Herla," she said in the voice of a woman much younger than she appeared, "There is no need to fret. Didn't you feel it at the Solstice? I know where

I am now. Everything is alright."

Without another word she slipped down from the saddle and on to the earth. As her feet touched the ground, a look of peace passed across her face and she closed her eyes. For just a moment, the ruin of two hundred years fell away, and a young woman in a white bal-maiden's skirt and apron stood before them with a smile of utter tranquillity on her lips, until shockingly, inevitably, she dissolved away to dust.

Chastity Trewartha was home.

26 DUST

The Lord of Misrule stood open mouthed in shock as he gazed at the spot where Chastity had just dismounted. The hunt did not react at all.

"What's the matter with you all?" He shouted in desperation. "Chastity just sacrificed herself, and you do nothing! You don't even appear concerned."

"I just told you," said King Herla, "it's over."

Understanding slowly spread across his countenance as The Lord of Misrule realised why the members of the hunt all looked so different.

"What happened to you at the Solstice?" he said. "What did Chastity mean when she asked if you felt it too?"

"We stopped time," replied Herla, "and when it was stopped something changed. We gained a sense of clarity that has been missing for centuries. All these years we have been riding as the hunt, caught up in the eternal chase, never thinking of anything else, but still yearning for the day we could dismount, and it was only when time stopped and I had time to think that I realised that the one thing I want when I can walk the earth is the one thing I can never have."

"And what exactly is that?" asked the Lord of Misrule.

"My wife," stated Herla. "There is only one place I am going to be reunited with her, and it's not in our world, or theirs."

At that moment, the bloodhound that been laying across the neck of Herla's horse languidly raised its head, and scented the air around it. Then, apparently satisfied that everything smelled right, it jumped down to the ground, and ran off through the snow, tail wagging furiously.

"Wait, so that's it," said the Lord of Misrule as he watched the bloodhound recede into the distance, "The hunt is over? You can dismount now and get on with your lives?"

"In a manner of speaking," replied Herla.

As if to prove Herla's point, another of the riders called over his hound, leant down from his horse and detached its leash. The animal barked once and ran off into the distance. The he too coiled his reins around the pommel and swung his leg over the top if his horse, lowered himself to the ground and dissolved away to dust.

More and more of the huntsmen repeated the same ritual. As they dismounted, the gentle breeze that had replaced the storm, caused their ashes to drift forward as they settled to the ground, giving the impression that the huntsmen we're sinking into the earth. Finally, only Herla was left, and then he too coiled up his reins.

"Wait", said the soon to be ex-Lord of Misrule, "what about me?".

"You'll be fine," said Herla, "If the centuries have taught me anything it's that all things pass. There will be another solstice."

"Not for you, and not for me either," replied the Lord of Misrule miserably "You can only be the Lord of Misrule once, I suppose that's it then."

Surprised by this turn of events, Liam walked towards the Lord of Misrule, placed a comforting hand on his shoulder and said "Oh, I wouldn't feel too bad about it. I mean, if the solstice didn't happen every year, you wouldn't have had the chance to be the Lord of Misrule in the first place, and anyway, you're going to be famous, they'll be talking about you for years."

"Hmm" replied the Lord of Misrule "I don't know that that is such a good thing - being remembered for being a failure."

"I don't think you'll be remembered as a failure. Misrule is the name of the game isn't it?" said Liam. "I doubt that anyone has ever turned things on their head quite as well as you did, you stopped time! What other Lord of Misrule has ever done that?"

"Yes, I suppose you're right. I will be famous won't I?" said the Lord of Misrule brightening, with much more of his earlier child-like charm.

Evan looked up as King Herla slowly urged his mount towards the brothers. The horse skittered slightly to one side, snorting, then settled again. Then, Herla turned in his saddle to Celyn who was still seated behind him, and said "My Lady?" as he offered her his forearm. Celyn took hold, and the king swung her down on to the ground that he still longed to walk upon. Celyn walked forward and joined Evan, Travis and Liam who had now grouped together again. King Herla raised his ancient corroded sword in front of him in salute, and the he too coiled up his horse's reins, and slowly and deliberately swung his leg over the saddle and lowered himself to the ground, and was gone.

Liam, Evan and Travis stood and looked at the empty place that until recently had been occupied by the fearsome Wild Hunt, until Celyn's voice broke through their thoughts.

"Come on," said Celyn. "Let's get going. It's a bit of a walk back up the hill back to your house, and there are a few more obstacles in our path now."

Without thinking, Liam and Evan turned and started to follow Celyn as she turned and began to trudge up the hill back towards their house.

"Wait, is that it?" asked Travis. "Is it really over?"

Despite the extremes of emotion they had been forced to endure over the course of the evening, the sudden conclusion felt just as unreal.

"I think so," said Celyn. "Things will certainly never be the same in the Otherworld without the Hunt. It will take a lot of getting used to."

They walked in silence as each member of the group tried to process the dramatic conclusion to the events of the day. As they made their way home the snow started to fall again, but this was not the intense whiteout they had experienced earlier. Certainly it lacked much of its earlier intense beauty, but it also lacked some of the sense of danger. Soon snow was settling all around them again, settling on their heads and shoulders, settling on the boughs of the trees, and the tops of the granite and slate walls and setting on the roofs of the houses they passed. And far behind them it settled over the tracks of the Wild Hunt and all the signs of struggle at the site of their conflict. It even settled over the hole left in the snow where Evan had plunged the Solstice Blade into the ground, and soon there was no sign of the old paper knife that lay buried up to the hilt amongst the trees.

"So what now Celyn?" asked Liam. "Is there any way back for you now the solstice has passed? Will you stay here?"

"For a little while, but I won't be here for long," she said. "Let's get back, and I'll tell you in the warm."

27 THE GIFT

Back in the house, things seemed to have returned to normality. The lights and clocks were back working as they always had done.

"Well, I suppose I'll have to try and find another present for Mum now," said Travis. "We'll never find the Solstice Blade again out there in the woods, and anyway, I'm not so sure I would want to give it as a present any more, not now that I know what it is."

"Yeah, it's probably for the best." added Evan, "The further that thing is away from temptation, human or otherwise, the better off we'll be if you ask me."

"I agree," said Celyn, "and I doubt it will ever be found now. When Evan plunged it into the earth we were still in the Otherworld. You have seen how time and place are different there. It could be anywhere in your world." Then turning to face Travis she said: "Now, about your mother's Christmas present." Raising her slender arms up level with her shoulders, she reached back behind her neck and continued, "have you considered jewellery?"

Celyn unclasped her necklace, and offered it to Travis, then added "it could be a gift from all of you."

"No way!" said Travis. "You can't give us your necklace. I mean it's beautiful, and mum would love it, but your father gave you that!"

"That's true," Celyn replied, "but had you three not helped me out he would have lost his daughter. I think I know which he'd rather keep hold of. I want you to give it to your mother. It's partly because of me that you lost your original gift after all. You know that holly is a symbol of eternal life don't you? Even in the deepest winter, when the days are at their shortest, and everything is frozen and cold, the holly remains bright, green and red and strong, defying the cold, and symbolising that life will always return."

Celyn placed the necklace in Travis's hand and closed his fingers over it. "Take it," she said. "I want your mother to have it. I think it would make a perfect gift, and she'll certainly never see anyone else wearing anything like it!"

"Well, ok, if you're sure. Thank you," said Travis.

"Yes, I'm sure," Celyn replied.

"Yes, thank you," said Liam and Evan simultaneously.

Travis's brothers gathered around him and they gazed down at the necklace laying in his open hand. It really was a beautiful thing, a simple sprig of holly with perfectly fashioned silver leaves that flashed as Travis turned it around in his hand. The blood red berries glowed with an inner light. The three brothers were absorbed in examining the necklace, and imagining how their mother would react when she received it, when Celyn spoke again.

"I'm glad that I had a chance to thank you for all you've done for me," she said.

Celyn's words had a strange finality to them, but it took a moment or two for Travis to realise that her voice also sounded somehow more distant than it had before. It wasn't that she sounded like she was further away, it was more that her voice was less 'present' in the room. He felt a sickening lurching feeling in the pit of his stomach, and as he looked up he was alarmed to see that Celyn was beginning to fade from view.

"No!" he called out, surprised by the unexpected note of panic he heard on his own voice.

Evan and Liam looked up too, concerned by the tone of his voice, and Evan called out almost involuntarily "Celyn, don't go!" as he too noticed that she seemed to be slowly becoming transparent.

In the space of a few seconds, everything had changed, and the brothers struggled to deal with the intensity of the feelings they were experiencing. Celyn's leaving created one of the strongest senses of loss they had ever known and it was all happening so fast, and so totally out of their control.

"I'm afraid I have no choice in the matter," replied Celyn with a hint of sadness. "The solstice has passed, and our worlds are drawing apart again. I can't stay: I'm not of this world."

Travis was the first to try and vocalise what they were all feeling, but none of them could explain. "But how will I, I mean we, how will we manage without you? I've never felt like this about anyone else."

"Try not to worry" said Celyn gently, "Even though you will soon be men, you are still young. What you feel for me is not what you think it is: it is the amplifying effect of the Otherworld again. In time you will meet someone from your world that you feel the same way about, so it's probably better that you will soon forget about me; it will spare you more anguish and pain"

"Wait, what?" Protested Liam, as her words sunk in. "We're going to forget? I don't want to forget, we don't have to forget do we?"

But even as she spoke them, the words began to fade from the brothers' memories, and they had to struggle to keep hold of them. It was like trying to recall upon waking something that was said in a dream, and with each passing second her words became more elusive.

"It's the way it has always been between your people and mine, and it's the way it must always be," she explained. "You'll have little flashes of memory, like when someone breaks a dream, but mostly you'll forget, and you will be fine."

"What?" said Evan.

"What do you mean, 'what?'" said Liam.

"Oh, nothing," replied Evan. "I thought you said

something, something about a dream." But now that he had said the words out loud he wasn't so sure anymore.

"Yeah, I thought so too" said Travis.

"Nope" said Liam, "I didn't say anything."

Travis had the strangest feeling that he had been in the middle of something, and had somehow become distracted, but it soon passed. And then as he looked around in a slight state of confusion he noticed that the film they had been watching had finished.

"Film's finished," he said, "I suppose I'd better get this necklace wrapped up for mum."

28 CHRISTMAS DAY

Liam awoke on Christmas morning and climbed out of bed. Drawing back the curtains, he looked out of his bedroom window. His gaze travelled out over the roofs of the houses that dropped away following the contours of the hill, and across the valley beyond. Overnight, a fresh covering of snow had fallen on top of that left behind by the unexpected blizzard of a few nights earlier. During the night the snow clouds had cleared away, and he now he found himself forced to screw up his eyes against the dazzling glare of the winter sun off the snow. For as far as he could see the world was pristine and clean and white. Only the Victorian viaduct stood out in stark contrast against the snowfield, carrying the railway across the valley, its tall, vertical pillars offering no surface for the snow to settle on. Even after having had a few days to get used to the idea that the snow looked like it was going to stay around until Christmas Day, he still found himself grinning at the view.

"Finally!" He said to himself. "A white Christmas in Cornwall - who'd have thought it?"

The snow really did seem to change everything. For the past few days Liam had felt much more festive than he had done in years, but this morning he felt a bubbling excitement building inside him that he thought he had lost for good as a child. Unable to contain the feeling he raced out of his room and along the hallway to Evan's room to wake him.

"Come on Evan!" he called, thumping on his brother's bedroom door as he passed. "Get out of bed; it's Christmas morning!"

"Christmas afternoon surely," came Evan's muffled reply, "must be if you're out of bed!"

Liam smiled to himself at the typically fraternal reply, and called back "and it's been snowing again," as he made his way down the stairs.

A short while later, most of the family had assembled in the front room.

"Seven thirty? Really?" Remarked Travis, as he wandered, in bleary eyed to join the rest of his family.

Liam grinned at Travis's remark. "You'll be fine in a moment," he said, "and then think how much of the day you'll have left. You'll thank me for getting you up this early!"

"Am I hearing this correctly?" asked their mother. "Shouldn't you lot be arguing by now? I was certainly expecting a bit more of a reaction than that from you Liam."

"Oh he's alright really," replied Liam playfully rubbing Travis's hair. For just a second, Liam though he remembered doing that in another time, in another place, when that one simple act meant that everything was ok again, but in another heartbeat the feeling was gone.

Despite their comments, Evan and Travis were actually feeling just as excited as their older sibling.

"Come on," said Travis, "let's open the presents. Mum, you go first. Evan, grab mum's present will you?"

Evan, happy for once to comply with his brother's wishes, retrieved a small box wrapped in brightly coloured paper from its position on top of the pile of packages arrayed beneath the Christmas tree, and walked over to where his mother was sitting on the settee. He was immediately joined by his brothers and all three of them crowded around her as Evan passed her the little parcel.

Their mother felt a little self conscious, at being so closely watched by her three sons, all eager to gauge her reaction to the gift that they had presented her with. Placing the parcel on her lap, she carefully released the tab of sticking tape that secured one of the folded ends of the paper to the side of the box, and unwrapped the gift. Inside was a small white cardboard box with a close fitting lid. Using one hand to steady the box, she rocked the lid from side to side with her other hand to free it, and then looked in. Inside lay a finely crafted silver pendant in the form of a sprig of holly. Sunlight glinted off the carved silver leaves. Somehow the craftsman who made it had managed to perfectly capture the waxy yet glossy texture of real holly. The cluster of blood red gemstone berries glowed as if they had absorbed the winter sunlight into themselves and it still burned deep within them. Encircling the holly sprig, and overlaid by some of the leaves was a circular band of silver engraved with letters.

"Oh my gosh!" said their mother, "I think that this is the most lovely thing I have ever seen! Thank you all so much."

Liam, Evan and Travis grinned in delight. They could not have been more pleased with their mother's reaction.

"Where on earth did you manage to find this?" asked their mother. "I don't remember you going out anywhere to buy it, and it doesn't look like the kind of thing you could have ordered online."

"We went into town on the night you and dad went to the theatre," said Travis; "we found it in that little second-hand shop on Fore Street."

Running her finger over the engraved letters, their mother read them out one at a time, "C, e, l, y, n" she said "Celyn, that's a lovely sounding word. I wonder what it means."

In moments, Evan had his phone in his hand, launched the web browser program, and conducted a quick search.

"It means 'Holly'," he said. "It's the Welsh word for Holly."

"If you spell it with a 'K'," said Travis surfacing from a web search of his own, "it's also the Cornish for 'Holly'".

"Here," said Liam, holding out his hand, "let me help you put it on."

Their mother lifted the pendant from the box, and was surprised to see a few white flakes fall from it and drift slowly down to the floor. She looked back into the box again, and noticed that the bottom of it was covered in a dusting of what looked rather like snow. That was ridiculous of course, any snow that might have accidentally got into the box would surely have long since melted away. Cupping her hand she tipped the box over, spilling its contents into her palm.

"This was a nice touch" she said, "putting fake snow into the box. Whose idea was that?"

"Not mine," said Travis. "I wrapped it, and I didn't put anything in there."

"Me neither," said Liam.

"Or me," added Evan.

Their mother took a pinch of the powder, and some of it melted instantly into little drops of water when it came into contact with her fingers.

"How strange, it certainly looks like snow," she said lifting the little box up in front of her face, so that she could examine it more closely. Then she turned it over and tapped the base a few times to dislodge the last few flakes, and allowed them to fall

Watching the snowflakes twist and pirouette on the warm currents of air in the room, each of the brothers found themselves gripped by an odd sensation. Like catching the unexpected scent of a familiar perfume, they felt a strong sense of dislocation, as if the wearer had just passed by but was nowhere to be seen.

The strange fragrance flowed through their minds, its intoxicating presence made them dizzy and subdued any resistance. The disorientating sensation grew stronger and stronger, until finally, irresistibly, it broke over them over them like a wave, and they were washed away from the present.

Although they knew that their feet were still on firm ground, and were surrounded by the familiar room, they also felt as though they were being drawn into a wild eccentric orbit around the falling flakes of snow. Their minds were transported back to a place of magic and cold and unlimited potential. The vertigo they were feeling was mirrored by the motion of the snowflakes, twisting and spinning them, dragging them inward to where every detail of each snowflake was crystal clear, and far more real than anything in this world had any right to be. The world smelled of ice and pine needles and excitement and unknown dangers. It was a feeling from a dream, bizarre and unreal, yet curiously familiar and compelling. And wasn't there someone..? A woman..? A person of incredible, unearthly beauty, whose very presence coursed through their veins, lighting fires and she was so, she was just so…

And just then, when they were on the very edge of remembering, the sensation receded like a wave pulling back from the shore, dragging and rolling the fragments of memory with it into the ocean of the past. And although the brothers fought its leaving with everything in their beings, it was unstoppable, and rapidly their wild orbit slowed, and the floor stopped tilting, until what remained was a room, in a house, surrounded by family, in a small Cornish market town, watching the last few snowflakes drifting earthward.

In the heat of the room, the snow never made it to the floor, and as they watched, one by one, the flakes disappeared, along with their memories of the curious event.

And outside, down in the valley, lost within in a copse of trees, an old silver paper knife was buried deep beneath the thick layer of snow that covered the ground. Hidden from view as it was, it would remain there frozen until the thaw. Even once the snow was gone it would still be barely visible under the canopy of trees, far from any road, with only the hilt protruding from the damp earth. Winter would pass and in the spring, vegetation would grow up around it disguising its location still further. In subsequent years it would be buried under layer after layer of autumn leaves, until it was eventually swallowed up by the earth never to be seen again.

Probably.

ABOUT THE AUTHOR

Rob Beck lives in Cornwall with his wife Paula and their three sons. He describes himself as an author, mandolin player and software engineer. The world at large tends to view this list the other way around, and renumerates him accordingly. Rob has two cats whom he has been known to turn to for inspiration, and although they are quite vocal in their response, their input has been found to be rather one-dimensional and often too cat-food related to be considered for inclusion in his novels.